The Hermit

a novel by
Ray Holland

THE HERMIT

ISBN-10: 0615279171
ISBN-13: 978-0-615-27917-6

Published by Great Big Dog
P.O. Box 161272
Louisville, KY 40256
www.greatbigdog.com

You can contact the author at greatbigdog@gmail.com with comments, suggestions, questions, or whatever. I can't promise to reply to all e-mail, but I'll read everything.

—RH

This novel is dedicated to the hermit and the mayor's daughter within each of us.

Acknowledgments

"Bashful" Jim Adkins, who, after reading a one-page synopsis way back once upon a time, suggested that the best way to write it would be as a humor piece.

Iverson Warinner and the rest of the folks in the theater department at Spalding College (now University), who staged the one-act play version of this story as part of their 1985 Old Louisville One-Act Play Festival.

Benjamin Hoff, whose book *The Tao of Pooh* had a small but important influence on the way I approached the characters when developing the play into a novel.

Kevin "The Kevinator" Thompson, for encouragement. It's all about the words, man. It's all about the words. Also Robbie Ritchie, Anna Halbert, and Justin Carver for reading and making suggestions.

TABLE OF CONTENTS

PART ONE: THE MAYOR'S DAUGHTER

CHAPTER ONE

Way far away from wherever it is that you happen to be, a hermit lived in a homemade shack on a mountainside.

This hermit lived in the usual hermit fashion, very simple and close to the earth. He grew vegetables in a little garden beside his shack and sometimes trapped small animals such as rabbits. "Oh, boy," he'd say when he trapped a small animal. "I'm going to have meat tonight."

Meat.

In the winter, he kept a nice little fire burning in his homemade fireplace, and outside he wore a coat he had made out of the furs of animals he had trapped. Just between you and me, I think the coat looked hideous. But really—who was going to see it?

He'd brought a few things with him when he started living on the mountainside. He had some books he read for intellectual fulfillment—or for entertainment. Or both. He also had some notebooks and pens so he could keep a journal of his spiritual journey of prayer and meditation. He wrote about things that happened to him, although living by himself on a mountainside in a forest meant that very little actually happened. It was an exciting day when he saw a cloud shaped like Woody Allen.

It was something to write about. He tried to imagine which movie it was from and decided it resembled Woody's character in *Manhattan*, looking the way Woody looks when he's standing there in that final scene talking to Mariel Hemingway. It happened three days in a row. Not the same cloud, because the clouds blew away each day. They were three different clouds, all shaped like Woody Allen in *Manhattan*. It was amazing. Another day would have been too much to bear. Fortunately the weather turned rainy, so the clouds weren't really shaped like much of anything on the fourth day.

"Dear journal," the hermit wrote, "it rained today, saving me from being overwhelmed by Woody." No one else would have understood that sentence. It's probably a good thing that no one else was around to read it.

Of course, our hermit had already been a hermit for a long time before Woody Allen ever made any movies. The *Manhattan* cloud story was just an example of the kind of things that happened to him.

Okay, so, let's see. We have the garden, trapping animals, meditating and praying, and keeping the journal. That's about it.

The hermit lived on the mountain for many years, doing his hermitstuff and mostly being content with his life. He had no problems with door-to-door salesmen because no one knew he was there, and he had no problems with telemarketers because he didn't have a phone. Who was he going to call when he didn't want to be around people anyway?

***

Eventually (about three or four years before our story takes place), some folks came along and built a little village at the foot of the mountain. It was a nice place for a village because it was near a river, and the ground was fertile, and so on and so forth. They didn't build the village just to irritate the hermit, but that was the way it seemed to him. He had been there for years, just grooving along with the universe—and then, all of a sudden, here were these daggone people building a daggone village! Of all the thousands of square miles of empty territory to choose from, they had to put their village right there under his nose, daggone it! Even around on the other side of the mountain would have been good enough, but no.

He was angry about it. Okay, so they didn't know he was there. But still...

There was the noise of the hammers and nails and the trucks bringing in the building materials and what-not.

Heavy on the whatnot. And the construction workers hooting and hollering and whistling at the pretty girls who walked by were a big distraction, too.

All that noise interfered with the hermit as he tried to do the stuff he was trying to do. He had been used to peace and quiet for many, many years, and now this.

He tried concentrating harder, but it didn't work. He tried stuffing leaves in his ears, but that just felt icky. After a couple of weeks, he started getting used to it. As time went on, first one building and then another was finished, and the noise gradually died down.

Then, one day, the rumbling and roaring and

hooting and hollering and whatnot were gone. The hermit found himself looking at a complete, brand-new, shiny, mint-condition village down at the foot of his mountain.

And although he didn't care for having a village so close, what could he do? It wasn't going to move, and he wasn't going to move. He could deal with it.

In spite of himself, he even enjoyed it just a little bit when the Exploding Sperm Whales played an outdoor concert one night. Besides that, he couldn't actually see the village from his shack. Lots and lots of forest was sitting in between.

***

Now, it just so happens that down in this village, there was a certain young lady, the mayor's daughter. She was twenty-one years old and very pretty, about five-five with shapely legs and a cute little button nose and long, wavy, black hair. That's how I picture her, anyway. If you want to picture her differently, go right ahead. The main thing is that she was pretty. The details don't matter.

The mayor's daughter was mostly a pretty good mayor's daughter. She had gotten good grades in school and was now working at the local animal shelter. She volunteered at the soup kitchen, helping feed folks who were down on their luck.

You would have been proud to have her as a daughter.

Except, as you may have noticed, she was "mostly" a good daughter, and that means there was a problem. The problem was that she...uh, well... Let's just say she enjoyed the society of gentlemen a little more than most folks thought she should.

You can interpret that any way you want. Let me say, though, that as far as I can tell, there's only one way to interpret it. I know what I would think.

The mayor's daughter didn't waste any time. The first day the local tavern was open, she was right in there, cruising for trouble.

She had her hair done up all fancy-like, and she was dressed in her most flattering outfit. She looked around, surveying the territory, checking out the guys. It didn't take her long to check out the guys because she was the first person there. She knew they would show up, though, and she would be ready. There was the bartender, of course, but she wanted to hold him in reserve. He would always be there.

She ordered a drink, a Howlatthemoon, all one word. It was the specialty of the house, inasmuch as a tavern can be said to have a specialty when it's served just one drink in its entire existence. It was nice and fruity. The drink, that is. Not the tavern.

The mayor's daughter sat down on a stool to sip on her drink. She gave the bartender a thumbs-up. He smiled at her. He was thinking nasty thoughts. He wanted to do all kinds of X-rated things to her. He wanted to commit unspeakable sexual atrocities and perversions upon her body.

But it would be unprofessional to tell her so.

The evening went on, and people came in.

The place was hoppin'. The jukebox was playing, and guys were shooting pool, and the mayor's daughter was deciding. She decided on a rugged-looking young fella who was in the corner playing darts. Thwap.

Thwap. Thwap. She ambled over, watching the game, sipping her drink, and sat down at a nearby table.

After the guy she liked finished his turn, she clapped. "That was very good," she said.

"Well, I do my best," the guy said.

"I'm sure you do."

And before he knew it, the guy was ensconced in a booth with the mayor's daughter, over on the other side of the room away from his friends. The two of them were talking and laughing. Her hand found its way onto his knee.

"Let's go someplace private," the mayor's daughter said.

"Where to you want to go?"

"Use your imagination."

Okay, so the guy wasn't too bright, but the mayor's daughter wasn't concerned. She didn't care about discussing nuclear physics or the finer points of Kant's *Critique of Pure Reason*. She needed him to know only one thing, and if he didn't know it already, he didn't have to be a genius to be able to learn it.

They went to his place. He had a swingin' bachelor pad a few blocks away. Well, it wasn't really anything like what you'd think of if someone asked you to picture what a swingin' bachelor pad is like. It was more like a room with some furniture in it. Now, of course, a swingin' bachelor pad is a room with some furniture in it, but you would describe it in much greater detail. You would talk about the revolving bed, the mirror on the ceiling, the 360-degree sound system, the well-stocked wet bar, and so on. Talking about this guy's place, about the only thing you can say was a room with some furniture in it.

It was good enough, though, to be a place where the mayor's daughter could commit unspeakable sexual atrocities and perversions upon this guy's body.

The neighbors complained about the noise. They complained about the banging and thumping and moaning and groaning and shouting and the electric motor sounds. What they didn't see, afterward, was the clothing strewn about the place, the furniture knocked over, the assortment of interestingly modified small kitchen appliances, medical devices and power tools, the food stains on the floor, the collection of specialized literature, and a number of other things I would be embarrassed to talk about.

The mayor's daughter made the most of her opportunities.

The guy couldn't go to work for the next two days. When he finally showed up, they had to put him on light duty for a couple weeks. He'd had a good time. He would have done it again, but not very soon. In the meantime he had a good story to tell.

And word got around.

***

Word didn't get to the hermit because he didn't talk to anyone. It did, however, get to the mayor. One of his assistants came into his office a few days later. "Sir, I hate to bring this up, but I think you'll want to know about it."

"What?"

"Well, uh..." The assistant was very reluctant to say it. How do you tell a guy his daughter has engaged in scandalous behavior so excessive and shocking that no more than three times since the close of the Middle Ages has anything like it happened on this plane of existence?

Also, this assistant had heard stories of crazed dictators who pulled out handguns and shot guys who brought them bad news. He didn't think it was likely the mayor would do something like that. Still, the idea was sort of knocking around in the back of his mind being worrisome.

"Well, uh..."

"Come on, out with it."

"There's a rumor going around about your daughter, sir."

"Yes?"

"It's not a good one."

"It's not?"

"No, sir. I'd go so far as to say it's bad."

"Well, tell me."

"Remember, sir, this is just a rumor. We don't have any evidence to prove it."

"I'll remember. Now tell me."

"Okay, sir, it's like this. There's an unsubstantiated rumor that your daughter met a certain young man at the tavern the other night..." And the assistant proceeded to tell the mayor all the sordid details. He told him about the banging and thumping, the moaning and groaning, the electric motor sounds, everything. He didn't hold anything back.

And at the end of the story the assistant stopped. He waited for the gun to come out. It didn't.

"Is that all?" the mayor asked.

"It's as much as we know."

The mayor nodded. He sat there a moment, behind

his desk, being the mayor, thinking about this awful story. He got up and strolled calmly over to a suit of armor that was standing in the corner as an ornamental thing. (Or maybe it wasn't just ornamental; one never knows when one might need a suit of armor. His daughter could have made good use of it with that guy she met.) And the mayor punched the suit of armor. It went clattering down, falling apart, making a huge racket.

The mayor's secretary opened the door. "Is everything all right?"

"Yes," the mayor said. "I, uh, I was just cleaning this suit of armor, and it went off."

"Yes, sir." She stood in the doorway, doing her best to look as if she were waiting for him to say something else, but was actually trying to figure out what was going on. She knew the mayor's excuse was bogus; the suit of armor wasn't loaded.

"You can go now," the mayor said.

She stood still.

"Really, you can."

She left.

The secretary was out of the room, but the problem was still right in front of the mayor. His daughter was misbehaving.

He—the mayor, that is—wished his wife were still with him. She had died a couple years earlier in a freak accident involving a thimble, a bag of croutons, and a backhoe from a construction site. A pair of tweezers might also have been involved. No one was ever able to figure out exactly what happened. The mayor—of course, he wasn't the mayor at that time—fell under a dark cloud of suspicion, but no one could prove anything. They couldn't prove anything because he had nothing to do with the accident. But they could still suspect him, and they did. That was largely why he came to live in this brand-new village at the foot of the mountain.

So the mayor wished his wife were still around. She would know how to deal with this problem. In fact, he was pretty sure that if she were still around, their daughter would never have engaged in such disgraceful behavior. She needed the guidance of a mother.

If only—the mayor thought—if only he were one of those crazed dictators who gunned down guys who told him stuff he didn't want to hear and had other guys drag the bodies out and dispose of them somewhere (who cares where?) so he could go on his merry way and pretend there was no problem.

He only thought that momentarily. He didn't really want to shoot anyone. He just thought it would be cool if, like, he could achieve the status of having shot someone without going through the unpleasantness of actually doing it. Or something. What was important was that the mayor knew he had to do something about the news his assistant had just told him. If not that, at least he had to appear to do something.

But what?

He'd figure it out. Maybe he could find a call-in radio talk show and ask about it. No, that wouldn't do. He didn't want to make it any more public than it already was. He would just read a book or look it up on a web site or somesuch.

Later.

Right now, he had to have lunch. He buzzed the intercom to call his secretary. "I'd like you to order me some unicorn stew from Dewey's Diner."

"Sir, I don't think they have unicorn stew."

"Well, ask whether they have it. If not, just get me a peanut butter and jelly sandwich."

CHAPTER TWO

The mayor tried to think about his problem. He wanted to, for real. Or he wanted to want to. What he did was spend the rest of the afternoon playing Universal Federation Wrestling on his Super Mega Game Console. He was pretty good at it. He played a character called The Lugubrious Barney and worked his way up to a championship match, which he lost. But he'd be back. Oh, you'd better believe it.

When you're the mayor of a village as small as this one, you have a lot of free time.

***

That night, the mayor sat down to dinner with his daughter. "How's it going?" he asked.

"Okay," she said.

"How…uh, how's your social life?"

"Okay."

"This sure is good lasagna."

"Yes, it is."

***

And after dinner, the mayor's daughter got the urge to socialize again. "I'm going out, daddy," she said.

"Where are you going?"

"I'm going to visit some friends."

"Have fun."

"I will."

She went to the tavern, sat down at the bar, and ordered another Howlatthemoon. The bartender made the drink, and because he had heard the story about her and the guy she had picked up—who hadn't?—he put a little extra vermouth in, just to show his appreciation. He didn't know what her intentions were, whether she just maybe wanted to sit and have a drink and relax, or if she was supposed to meet the same guy, or if she was on the prowl for another guy, or what. Of course, she still had her eye on the bartender, but remember, she was keeping him in reserve. So she sat there watching guys coming in and drinking and socializing with their friends and going back out.

A good number of people had heard the story about that first guy—or to put it more accurately, a good number of people had heard some version of the rumor. A few people were walking around town believing that the apartment building had burned down as a result of her sexual excesses and that the residents were lucky to escape with their lives. One guy had even been told, although he wasn't sure whether to believe it or not, that a portal to another universe had opened up in the closet of that guy's apartment and a number of strange and exotic creatures had joined in the merrymaking.

Some of the guys in the tavern had heard various forms of the story, and they did whatever they thought would catch the mayor's daughter's attention. They smiled at her, they looked at her with smoldering, seductive gazes, they sent her drinks. Some tried to look cute. Some puffed their chests out trying to look studly. One guy went to the men's room and stuffed wads of toilet paper down the front of his pants. He came back out with a lumpy, unsightly bulge that made him look deformed. A lot of the guys who hadn't heard any version of the story were also trying to get her attention simply because she was an attractive young lady.

The mayor's daughter talked to a few of them—just a little bit of harmless chit-chat. Then she made up her mind and decided which guy she wanted.

They went back to his place and created a new rumor. Again there was excessive noise, bumping, thumping, and so on. The building shook. Body fluids were flung about the room with gleeful abandon. There were utensils, appliances, modified power tools, blow-up dolls, chanting, costumes, and intense heat radiating from an unknown source.

The guy ended up happy. The mayor's daughter ended up happy.

She snuck home early the next morning before the mayor got up, and she went to bed.

***

A couple days later, the mayor's daughter was doing her volunteer work at the soup kitchen, side by side with her best friend. The new story, about her adventures with the second guy, was making its rounds around town. Some of the down-on-their-luck men were leering at her. Some of the down-on-their-luck women were giving her cold, disapproving looks. A few of the down-on-their-luck people were whispering to other down-on-their-luck people and pointing at her.

If you had been standing close to some of these whisperings, you might have heard words and phrases like "farm-fresh produce," "wading pool full of chocolate pudding," "secret cache of uranium 235," and so on. Once again, the story had gotten exaggerated as it circulated. And it's easier to exaggerate a story when no one knows what really happened. "Hey, man, you know what? The guy who operates the drill press down to the fabrication plant, he said they were doing something with six dozen pairs of football shoulder pads. Those real bulky kind, like the linemen wear."

Who could say any different?

And just in case you're wondering, the guys she had played with weren't doing anything to deny anything or tone down the rumors. Of course, the true stores of those adventures, just plain and unadorned, would have been wild and excessive enough to immortalize those guys forever as heroes in the annals of the sexual exploits of the village guys, but you know how young men are. If you don't, trust me: that's how they are. Some of them.

But letting the stories run with unchallenged exaggeration didn't hurt anything, as far as they were concerned. In fact, it lent the stories an air of being legendary.

What young man wouldn't love to be renowned as a sexual legend? Even the hermit (Remember the hermit? We'll get back to him.), in his days as a strong, young man, might have relished such a reputation. Even now, fifty years a hermit, he would enjoy thinking, if he had some reason to think so, that a group of old men might be sitting around somewhere talking about the sexual exploits of their younger days, and they might recount stories of that one guy…who was he? He hasn't been seen around town for fifty years; rumor has it he became a hermit or something, but no one's sure. But oh, my gosh, the stories about that guy! Folk ballads have been written about him….

But that's neither here nor there. Right now we're still at the soup kitchen, with the mayor's daughter and her best friend serving up dinner to the down-on-their-luck folks, and some of the down-on-their-luck folks have been spreading rumors about her.

The mayor's daughter knew what they were doing. She wasn't stupid; she knew exactly what was going on. Now, she would have to allow as how this wasn't the most pleasant thing that could happen right there in front of her, with folks whispering behind their hands and pointing and such. On the other hand, she didn't let it bother her too much. She was very self-assured. She was, by golly, going to live life on her own terms, and if other people couldn't mind their own business, or if they didn't like what she was doing, well, that was their problem. They could just go bite a big one.

"You know what these people are talking about, don't you?" the mayor's daughter's friend asked.

"I have a pretty good idea."

"You don't care?"

"It would be silly to worry about it, wouldn't it?"

The friend stopped serving for a moment and looked at the mayor's daughter. She wasn't sure what to say. "You mean you don't care?"

"Do you think I should stop doing what I want to do because someone else doesn't approve? I'm not hurting anyone."

"You tell 'em, young lady," said the old man waiting to be served.

The mayor's daughter glanced at him. He leered at her. "I would turn you inside out," she said.

He kept on leering.

"Literally," she said.

He kept on leering.

"I'm using the word 'literally' correctly," she said. "Not in the incorrect sense that most people use it, when they just want to emphasize their point. I'm saying I would turn you inside out, not as a metaphor for some sort of strenuous activity, but literally. You would end up with your guts on the outside of your body. The rest of your life would be a waking nightmare. The only saving grace would be that you couldn't live very long that way."

He digested that bit of info, and the leer faded. He took his tray and moved on.

"I'm just saying," the friend said, "you have to live among these people. That means you have to compromise somewhere to get along with them. We all do."

"Okay, my compromise is that I don't care if they talk about me. So what?"

***

Meanwhile, the new story was reaching the mayor. His assistant came into his office, all nervous-like and such. He clearly didn't want to do this. He didn't want to be there at all. He wished, devoutly, that he could at that moment be working as a roadie on a Neil Diamond tour. Not only would he not have to break bad news to his boss, but he could see interesting places like New York and Germany and Las Vegas and...well, lots of places.

But he was here. "Sir?" the assistant said timidly.

The mayor put his Interstellar Football Association computer game on pause. Various alien life forms wearing bulky body armor were frozen in an interesting tableau of running and blocking and arm waving and eye gouging. "Yes, what is it?"

"Uh, well, sir, it's like this. I, uh...well..."

"Is this another rumor about my daughter?"

"I'm afraid it is."

They mayor blinked and sighed. "Same guy or a different one?"

"Different."

"More lurid, less, or the same?"

"More, sir. It would seem she's stepping up her game."

"Stepping up her game? What the heck is that supposed to mean?"

"I don't know, sir. I'm just here to tell you the bad news."

"I don't want to hear about it."

"Are you sure? I know it's not pleasant, but maybe you need to know what people are saying."

The mayor sighed. He had a third and five on his own thirty-three yard line, down six points. "All I need to know is that there's a rumor going around," he said.

"Yes, sir."

Whether he *needed* to know the details or not, he didn't *want* to hear them.

***

And other people who didn't want to hear about it were the leaders of the mayor's political party. At headquarters, the party chairman was busy being disgusted. "I don't like hearing this," he said. "It's bad."

"Yes, it is," his secretary said.

"This is already well on the way to becoming a major scandal," the chairman said. "It's clear that she's going to make a habit of this, and it's only going to get worse and worse. This is the sort of thing that loses elections."

"But the mayor has only been in office a few weeks. The election's a long way off."

That was true, but it didn't make the situation any the less serious. Here's what the chairman was thinking: He was thinking that this situation could go in one of two directions. The bad direction was that if the mayor's daughter was allowed to continue what she was doing, then by the time the election came, the opposition could point to four years of wild, disgraceful behavior and the mayor's inability to make her behave.

The good direction would be to somehow make her stop, and soon. Then, when the election came around, they could pretend it had never happened. If the opposition said anything about it, the mayor could say, "Yeah, we had this little problem early in my first term, but I dealt with it, and everything's been peachy keen since then." Yeah, that would make him sound like a man who could get things done.

"Well, I'm sure the young men of the town could easily be persuaded to vote for the mayor again," the secretary said.

"That's not going to be enough. No, we have to take

action. Let's see...what's the first thing we need to do?"

"Tell the mayor to make his daughter behave?"

"No, that's the second thing. The first thing is to hire a public relations company to spin this thing."

"I don't think there are any public relations firms in town, sir," the secretary said.

"Then get me an appointment with one of those fancy New York firms and book me a flight. Tell them this is an emergency. We don't have a minute to spare."

***

The party chairman flew to New York that night and was able to meet with one of the partners of the fancy PR firm the next morning. The firm had been booked up for months in advance—that was how the chairman's secretary knew they were good—but the secretary told them there was a secret cache of uranium 235 in the village, and if they didn't win the next election it would fall into the hands of nefarious evildoers. And so one of the partners in the firm cleared out his schedule for the next day so he could meet with the party chairman.

That secretary, she was really on the ball.

The chairman and the partner met in the conference room at the firm's headquarters. Ordinarily the partner would meet with clients in his office, or in the client's office, but this was a matter of such grave concern that it couldn't be discussed anywhere but the conference room. It was a big place, with a long table in the middle of the floor and a big window at one end of the room and a movie screen at the other end. The movie screen was supposed to be for business-related presentations and such, but mostly they used it to watch

Bugs Bunny cartoons.

The chairman and the partner sat at opposite ends of the table so as to feel they were making the fullest use of the facilities, but it quickly became apparent that they were too far apart. So they just went up to the partner's office.

The chairman told the partner his story, all about the mayor's daughter and the guys and the modified power tools and the costumes and explosions and robots (I hadn't mentioned the robots, had I?) and whatnot, and the stories going around town and the people—most of them, that is—disapproving of her behavior.

"We plan to get the girl to stop all this fooling around," the chairman said. "But we also need some way to spin all this so it doesn't look so bad."

The partner nodded. "Of course," he said. "Of course. Let us work on it for a while and see what we can come up with. I'll let you know."

***

Meanwhile, another party official was meeting with the mayor. "You have to control your daughter," the official said.

"I know."

"You have to make her stop this promiscuous behavior."

"I will."

"Do you have any idea how you can do that?"

"No, I don't." Hey, at least he was honest.

"Can you explain things to her and make her understand the error of her ways? Will you have to threaten her? What will it take?"

Well, the mayor would rather explain than threaten. "I'll explain it to her," he said. He tried to sound confident.

"Good. I'm glad we had this little talk."

"So am I."

***

And in New York, the PR people were brainstorming. In the conference room.

"I think we should say she was possessed by evil spirits."

"I think we should say she was kidnapped and replaced by a lookalike."

"It was someone else, a case of mistaken identity."

"It was really a robot."

"Keep the ideas coming," the partner said.

***

A couple days later, the mayor's daughter dragged another lucky guy off to commit excessive sexual atrocities, which made the mayor realize the urgency of talking to her. Unfortunately, he couldn't think of anything that would be good to tell her, that he thought would be effective. So he just decided to improvise. "Daughter, come here," he said authoritatively when she came home from her job at the animal shelter.

"Yes, daddy?"

"It, ah...ahem...has come to my attention that you've been misbehaving with boys."

"Well, daddy, that depends on your definition of

misbehaving."

"When you're the father of an attractive young lady," the mayor said, "you generally have a pretty strict definition of what misbehaving means."

"Okay."

"I've heard stories."

"I think they've been exaggerated."

"Well, now, that makes it even worse than it really is, doesn't it?"

"I don't see how, daddy. It doesn't mean I did stuff I didn't really do."

The mayor wasn't expecting that. He didn't even understand it. So he plowed forward. "The point is," he said, "that you've been doing things you shouldn't be doing. You have to stop."

"I do?"

"Yes."

"Why?"

"Because you shouldn't be doing those things."

"What's wrong with it?" she asked. "I'm not hurting anyone."

"Well, you see, that's where you and I disagree. Maybe you're getting a momentary thrill, but in the long run it's meaningless." It was a real stretch for him to use a word like "momentary."

"It doesn't have to be meaningful," she said.

"Then there's another thing. People are talking."

"So what? I don't care."

"That's okay, except that me being in my position, as mayor of the village, it's a political problem."

"Why? You're not doing anything they disapprove of."

"But I'm not stopping you from doing stuff they

disapprove of. When the next election comes, that looks bad for me."

"But daddy, the next election is a long way away."

"If you don't stop all this fooling around, then by the time the next election comes, people will see you've been misbehaving for almost four years."

"Okay, but I just have to be me. I'm trying to have some fun, daddy. Take advantage of my youth."

"Can't you take advantage of your youth by, oh, I don't know, maybe going to the movies or something?"

"I can go to the movies after I get old."

"Then join a women's basketball team."

"Daddeee..."

"I'm just saying, daughter, that other girls are perfectly happy behaving themselves, not doing all sorts of promiscuous stuff. Why not you?"

"Well, gosh, everybody can't be the same."

"Just try, okay? Just try. If I don't get reelected, then I'm out of a job. You wouldn't want that, would you?"

"There are lots of other things you can do. You could become a hair stylist or a flute teacher."

"I hate to admit this, but I can't do anything else. I'm totally incompetent. If I can't be the mayor, I have no idea what I could do."

Now, don't get the wrong idea. It might sound as if the mayor's daughter didn't care about her daddy's predicament, but that wasn't the case. She understood, and she sympathized. But she just didn't have it in her to change her ways. She wanted to sample everything life had to offer in that particular area. She didn't want to promise something she didn't think she could do.

And yet she sat there looking at him, and he was so

upset, so distraught. It broke her heart to see him that way. Well, maybe it didn't actually break her heart, but it gave her unpleasant little twinges, to be sure. Also, this conversation had already gone on far too long for her liking, and she was pretty sure she wasn't going to get out of it until she told him something he wanted to hear. "I'll try, daddy," she finally said, hoping it would be good enough. "I'll try to behave myself."

"You need to do more than try," he said.

"Daddy, you have to understand, I can't change just like, like..." she snapped her fingers, "that."

"Yes, of course. That would be too much to expect. But you'll try, won't you?"

"I promise." She kinda sorta wanted to promise to try—for him. As far as a *real* try, her heart wasn't in it. She just hoped she sounded sincere.

The mayor let himself be convinced. If he had been able to look at the scene objectively, to coolly evaluate what was going on, he would have figured it out. How could he not? As it was, he didn't want to think about it too much because that would be, like, all uncomfortable and stuff. He had that nagging little doubt in the back of his mind, but it was easy to ignore.

***

And in New York, at the big fancy PR firm, the brainstorming was still going on.

"We can say it's a case of mistaken identity."

"Maybe we can say she was just studying with them."

"That's a dumb idea."

"Now, guys, remember, when you're brainstorming

there's no such thing as a dumb idea."

"Maybe not, but when we're finished brainstorming, it'll become dumb."

"Your mama's dumb."

"If you can't be any more creative than that, you shouldn't be working here."

"Oh, go to heck, poopie-pants."

***

As the next couple weeks passed, the owner of the tavern noticed something. He noticed that business from the young men of the village would steadily go up for a few days until the mayor's daughter came in to find a playmate. The next day business dropped sharply, but it would then gradually build up again. It was a regular thing.

***

Meanwhile, the hermit was going about his ordinary hermitlife. His ultimate spiritual goal was to reach, by means of meditation and contemplation, the High Plane of Astral Everythingness, where One is in Harmony with the All and the All is in Harmony with One, and Everything is Indistinguishable from Everything Else.

He had made a lot of progress over the years. All in all, the journey would consist of 143 steps. He had breezed through the first seven steps quickly and easily. It seemed so easy that he was a bit disappointed. He'd gotten that far and didn't feel he had actually accomplished anything.

But after that, it became more challenging. It was more complex.

Steps eight through thirty-four were tougher, and they had indeed left him with some sort of feeling of accomplishment. Step thirty, the State of Sensible Beingness, was particularly fun, as it involved playing Chinese Checkers with puppies.

He felt he was making progress—not just in terms of the number of steps he had achieved, but in learning profound and true things about the universe and his place within it. For example, he had learned that Chihuahua puppies were cutthroat Chinese Checker players, but Dobermans weren't very good at all.

He stopped for a couple weeks and rested at number thirty-four. That one, by the way, was called the Supreme Meaning of Ethereal Condensation. He liked it there. It was a nice place to hang out for a while, very pleasant. The humidity was just right.

But he had to move onward. He worked his way upward, through more steps, some easy, some difficult, stopping a couple more times to rest his spiritual muscles and then moving on.

At the time our story takes place, the hermit had just finished step 135. Yes, he was that close—*that close*—to reaching the final step of enlightenment. He had only eight steps to go. Yes, he was in the single digits, daddy-o. Single digits.

Step 135 had been the most difficult of all. Oh, my gosh. It was the Preying Bird of Eternal Midnight, and it was aptly named. It was very dark—not so dark that you'd open your eyes and see nothing but blackness, but very shadowy, with a disconcerting lack of color and detail. It had a slight chill; the equivalent in the physical world would be weather that's just cold enough to make you think about putting on a sweater before leaving the house, and there would be a slight breeze, just strong enough to make you feel the discomfort is being insistent.

He was there for almost a year, at the Preying Bird of Eternal Midnight. He was stuck. At first he relished the challenge. Then he became tired, and then worried that he wouldn't make it through. Then he panicked and floundered about for a while. Then he decided to stop. He just gave up. Step 135 was pretty far along; it was a lot farther than most people got, so maybe he should think of it as being good enough. He lingered there for two and a half months, not trying.

Just as a side note, I should make it clear that all this stuff about things that happen during the journey—the puppies and the constant darkness, and whatnot—all that is just stuff that the seeker (in this case the hermit) experiences during meditation sessions. When he's not meditating, in normal everyday life, things are just as you would expect them to be for a guy who has been living all alone for decades with no television set.

Anyway, the hermit was having problems at the Preying Bird of Eternal Midnight. It was common knowledge among hermits that most found similar difficulties in their spiritual journey. The problems, and the steps at which those problems appeared, varied considerably. Other hermits breezed through the Preying Bird of Eternal Midnight in as little as fifteen minutes. On the other hand, our hermit had found step seventy-six, the Rising Form of Actuality, to be his easiest. He had breezed through it while eating lunch one day. Yet no fewer than a dozen other hermits were stuck there indefinitely. Or so he had heard.

Some had big problems in as many as six or eight steps along the way. Some remained at a bad step for ten years or more. Some even gave up and languished in hopeless despair for the rest of their lives at whatever step they happened to be stuck.

It was rare—extremely rare—for anyone to go through all the steps without facing the existential angst of at least one level that seemed impossible.

The folks at hermit school even taught the students about this in the first semester. They wanted to make sure the students understood how it could be, in case they wanted to back out before devoting too much time to the hermit career path. Very few backed out, though. Like having kids, it was the sort of thing you don't truly understand until it happens.

So he wasn't the only one to face the problem of a step that seemed impossible. It was common. But that didn't help him get through it. He was all by himself, which is the main point to becoming a hermit.

And so he sat, all alone, with no clue as to how he was going to make any further progress.

Yet the atmosphere—the spiritual atmosphere—at that step was, as we've already seen, too oppressive to remain there indefinitely. And what made it worse was that this was the period when they were building the village at the foot of the mountain.

The hermit gathered his wits and evaluated his position as best he could. To lift himself out of the depths of the Preying Bird of Eternal Midnight would require dedication, devotion, and discipline. This was serious business.

He meditated and wrote in his journal. He read. He fasted. He exercised. He went on incredible internal journeys. He figured out how to play "The William Tell Overture" by cracking his knuckles.

He was not going to fail.

And along about the time the final building of the brand-spanking-new, mint-condition village was completed—in fact, on the very day the mayor took the oath of office—the hermit found his way out of the Preying Bird of Eternal Midnight. What he hadn't noticed, not in all that time he was stuck, was that a trap door was set in the floor just inside the entrance. One look down would have solved the whole thing.

And he was now on the Bridge of Constant Focus. It was a much nicer place.

Yet something was not quite right. As he stepped across the frontier from the Bird of Eternal Midnight to the Bridge of Constant Focus, he caught a glimpse, an oh-so-brief glimpse out of the corner of his eye, of a very pretty young lady off in the distance. She had shapely legs and a cute little button nose and long, wavy, black hair. At least he thought that was what she looked like. He hadn't gotten a good enough look to be sure.

The hermit turned and gazed off in the direction where he had seen her, but she wasn't there anymore. He had an urge to go chase her, to find her, to ask what she was doing there. She didn't belong in his spiritual journey.

But then, he thought, it didn't matter. She had seemed wholesome and not at all threatening. Besides that, she was gone now.

CHAPTER THREE

In New York, the PR firm had decided on the best way to spin the scandal. They were going to accuse the guys who had been playing with the mayor's daughter of working with the opposing party. They, the PR people, were going to say that these rumors, these scandalous stories about the mayor's daughter's behavior, were all a great big stinky bunch of lies designed to discredit the mayor.

They even set up a "dummy" PR firm, a fake company that would take the fall. There would be evidence that the other New York PR firm (the dummy firm), working with the opposing party in the village, had manufactured the whole thing, the entire scandal, in their conference room.

The people of the village would eat it up. A first-rate political scandal that involved a conspiracy would easily trump a second-rate sex scandal that involved a girl who merely wanted to have a good time.

The PR firm presented their idea to party officials, complete with charts and a multimedia presentation. The mayor and the chairman of the party agreed. Great idea, they said.

The campaign was to start with an anonymous

tipster identifying himself as an intern at a fancy New York PR firm (the fake one) leaking an e-mail to the village's television station. So word went out through the usual channels that the firm (the real one) needed writers for a special, top-secret project. Hundreds answered the call. They sent resumes and writing samples and so on and so forth. This was going to be a peach of a job, and the pay was daggone good.

It was highly competitive. The stakes were high, so none but the best would do for this job.

After reading and evaluating all the writing samples and interviewing the candidates, the PR firm finally hired the five best writers. The five writers were all going get the same assignment, and the PR firm was going to use the best work they submitted.

And while the writers were at work, the PR firm set up the fake, competing fancy New York PR firm as the place where the e-mails were supposed to come from. They rented an office in the basement of an abandoned warehouse somewhere in New York City. They installed a phone and set up a computer and hired a secretary-type to sit at a desk. If someone called, it would appear to be real—real and legitimate. If, however, someone showed up at the office to take a look, it would become pretty well clear that the whole thing was a put-on.

But they were sure that no one from the village would go to New York City. Hey, it gave the party chairman the heebie-jeebies when he went, but he couldn't see any way to avoid it.

Okay, so anyway, the writers turned in their work, and the big, fancy New York PR firm chose the best e-mails to use in their devious, evil plan.

The phone answerer in the basement fired up her computer and typed in the first message, addressing it to the TV station in the village.

***

One of the interns was the first to read it. "Holy smoke," he said breathlessly. "This is big."

The intern went to get his supervisor and showed him the e-mail. "Holy smoke," the supervisor said. "You're right. This is big."

The supervisor went to get the head of his department. "Holy smoke," the department head said. "This is more than big. This is *really* big."

And so the e-mail went up through the chain of command, through the manager and the department director and the administrator and the vice president and on up to the Head Guy In Charge of Everything.

They wasted no time. Well no more time, that is, other than the time it had already taken to show all these people this e-mail that had come in. They held a meeting (in the conference room, no less) and decided it was big, a big scandal in the making, and that it should be the lead story on that night's show.

And so it was.

"We begin tonight with a political scandal in the making," the anchor said. "Earlier today an inside source forwarded an e-mail to us outlining a plot to discredit the mayor."

On the screen, a graphic with the text of the e-mail appeared:

Dear opposing party chairman,

You'll be pleased to know that our plans to discredit the mayor are almost complete. We've hired a staff of highly qualified writers to write stories about how the mayor's daughter is misbehaving. Even as I write this note, they're hard at work creating horrible, scandalous stories that'll amaze and astound you. These stories will thrill you and chill you; they'll make you laugh and cry. They'll make your heart stop beating, but not for long enough to kill you.

.... Tomorrow, we start auditioning guys to spread these stories around the village as rumors. We're going to screen them very carefully to make sure they're both immoral and amoral, and to make sure they'll relish playing a part in a deviously evil scheme such as this.

It won't be long before the mayor is forced out of office in disgrace. HA HA HA HA HA HA HA!!!!!

It's a shame that the mayor's daughter will have her reputation ruined in this evil plot because really she's such a nice, wholesome, virtuous (heavy on the virtuous) young lady, but POLITICS ARE POLITICS. If innocent people are ground underfoot as we ruthlessly pursue our evil ends, so much the better. HA HA HA HA HA HA HA!!!!!

"This plot is evil," the anchor said. "We'll follow up with more details of this shocking, evil story as we get them."

At party headquarters, the party chairman turned off the TV and sat back. "Very good," he said to the other party officials. "The plan is in motion. All we have to do now is hope the mayor's daughter can behave herself."

Yeah, well, you probably already know how that went, right?

***

Right.

The mayor's daughter was also watching the news on TV. She was sitting on the sofa with her best friend, unable to believe what she had just seen. "How could anyone tell such lies?"

"You mean you really haven't been playing around with those guys? You've really been wholesome and virtuous?"

"Oh, don't be stupid. I've done all that stuff. It's the news report that's a lie."

"But they couldn't put it on television if it weren't true!"

"They just did, best friend. They just did. Something funny's going on around here, and I'm going to find out what it is."

"Why are you so upset about it? They're saying you're virtuous. If I were you, I'd just take it and let it drop."

The mayor's daughter didn't have a reply to that.

***

The mayor's daughter wasn't the only one who wanted to know what was going on. The chairman of the opposing party had seen the news story, and he was livid, livid with rage. He stalked around the house, stomping his feet, cursing and waving his arms. His face was red. Steam was shooting out of his ears. You may think I'm making up the steam just for comic effect, but steam was really shooting out of his ears. Don't ask me how. And if you happened to be there, you would think you were watching a cartoon.

He called all his fellow party officials, cronies, assistants, and so on. This was a bad story. A bad, bad story, and they had to do something about it.

This was an emergency.

They met at opposing party headquarters. One of the cronies had just happened, by coincidence, to tape the news show because they were running a story about the local elementary school and his child had been interviewed. "I wanna grow up to be just like my daddy," the kid had said.

Misguided though it is to want to grow up to be just like a political crony, it was a good thing the kid said it. The news reporter liked the quote so much—more for the way the kid said it than what he actually said—that she promised to make sure they'd use it on TV. So proud daddy taped the show. What parent wouldn't want to preserve a quote like that? And as a result he also got the emergency-inducing segment on tape as well.

Opposing party headquarters was equipped lavishly. They had an indoor swimming pool. They had a billiard room, a video arcade, a four-lane bowling alley, and a tea shop for some reason named after a character from a classic American novel. Pretty daggone nice. But no one was interested in any of those things. What they were interested in was the state-of-the-art home theater system, where they could watch the offending news segment over and over.

Which is exactly what they did. Over and over, so much that everyone ended up memorizing it. They discussed it, analyzed it, asked one another questions, and brainstormed ideas as to how such a thing could have been reported.

"We all know that this plot, if it's true, is nothing our party would ever, or could ever, condone. I mean, I think we all know that this is far too unethical even for us."

There was a general murmur of agreement among the fellow opposing party officials, assistants, and cronies.

"But," the chairman continued, "what if someone took it upon himself to do this on his own? What if we have a loose cannon in our midst?"

There was a general murmur of surprise and shock among the opposing party officials, assistants, and cronies. Yes, it was possible, maybe, perhaps...but who wanted to think about something like that?

"We have to think about something like that," the chairman said. "It might not be true. I hope it's not true. But the fact is, right now we just don't know. These things have been known to happen."

More analysis, more brainstorming. The chairman finally adjourned the meeting at about three in the morning. But he kept his two most trusted advisors longer.

"You're the only two people I'm certain I can trust," he said. The advisors beamed in delight. In a dark room, you could have read a book in their glow.

"I want to hire a private investigator to find out whether someone in our party might have done this," the chairman said. "And if it wasn't an opposing party member, then who was it?"

The trusted advisors nodded wisely. They agreed that it was a good idea. They needed to know where that story had come from.

***

Who else was interested in that news report? You might think the young men of the village would be, but you would be wrong. Yeah, sure, they were interested to the extent that they talked about it among themselves a little bit, but not a whole lot. They'd say stuff like, "Did you see that news story about the rumors about the mayor's daughter?"

And the other guy would say something like, "Yeah, ain't that something?"

That was about as far as it went. Those who had actually played with the mayor's daughter knew something funny was afoot, that someone was obviously lying for some reason, but hey, that was politics. It was dirty business, much nastier than promiscuous sex could ever be.

But so what? They'd had their fun. And if she wanted, there was no reason not to go for more. If people were saying on the news that she was virtuous, then it would be easy for the guys to deny that they had ever misbehaved with her—if, for some reason, it might become necessary to deny something.

***

In the village, people were abuzz. As we've already said,

a first-rate political scandal that involves a conspiracy trumps a second-rate sex scandal that involves a girl who merely wants to have a good time. (For a first-rate sex scandal, you have to have adultery and/or bigamy and/or the actual public figure him- or herself doing something he or she shouldn't. A single, unattached family member being a little too active doesn't cut it.)

This political scandal, as far as political scandals go, was fair-to-middlin', as they say. The public could see very clearly that there was some sort of power struggle going on behind the scenes. If the news report was true, then someone powerful had been lying to them. If it wasn't, then someone else who was powerful was lying to them. Either way, it was a field day for the cynics, and the uncertainty gave the paranoid-minded something to think about.

***

And the hermit? Well, he didn't know any of this was going on. He had no reason to care about it.

***

The mayor's daughter sat in her room, thinking. She sure was curious about that TV news report. Now, on the one hand, her best friend had a point when she had said that if they wanted to say she was virtuous, she should just let it go at that. Yeah, virtuous. If people believed it, what was the problem? That was what daddy wanted, anyway.

Hmmm...what daddy wanted.

Could he have had something to do with this?

It was certainly reasonable for her to entertain the idea, but of course he hadn't had anything at all to do with it. The chairman had kept the mayor out of the loop on purpose. If that fool knew it was actually a PR campaign, he'd do something to screw it up.

For sure.

***

The hermit continued meditating at the Bridge of Constant Focus. His consciousness walked across the bridge, occasionally stopping to look over the railing so as to check out the view of the horizon (gorgeous, I might add, with the river winding away into the distance, looking as if it were flowing into the setting sun).

The hermit didn't know where this bridge was. Well, it was on a spiritual plane; he knew that. But spiritual planes can be tricky places to nail down, and very often they're associated with some sort of physical space. This bridge might be modeled on a place in, say, Louisiana, or in Africa, or just about anywhere. He supposed that if he knew more about vegetation, what plants grew in what areas, he would have a better idea.

Ultimately, though, it didn't matter. If it did, he wouldn't be there. The idea was simply to get across the bridge.

Up ahead, he saw a brown paper bag on a dinner table that was placed in the middle of the bridge. He approached the table and looked inside the bag. Cookies. Lots of different types of cookies. Chocolate chip cookies, sugar cookies, Oreos, shortbread cookies, peanut butter cookies, oatmeal cookies, biscotti, a variety of Girl Scout Cookies (including his favorite kind, the chocolate mint, which of course he hadn't had since before he left civilization to become a hermit), even a few brownies and some pfeffernusse. And others. I just don't care to sit here and type out the names of a bunch more cookies, and I'm sure you don't care to sit there and read them. We'll just say there were a bunch more. Whatever your favorite is, some of them were in the bag.

Now, the hermit intuited that he shouldn't eat all the cookies. He was pretty sure this was a test. Who was administering the test, he didn't know. It didn't matter. If it was there in front of him, it was there for a purpose. He knew he didn't have to actually eat anything in the meditative world, so the cookies must be metaphorical.

Yes, metaphorical cookies. But daggone, they sure looked good. He thought it might be a psychological test, like, say, you choose a cookie, and your choice indicates something about your personality. Maybe if he picked up an oatmeal cookie, it would show that he was wise beyond his years. And then again, it could be dangerous. If he picked, for example, a sugar cookie, someone might take it as an indication that he was mentally unbalanced.

He had to be careful which cookie he selected.

Or maybe he could select more than one? What if he took the whole bag? Maybe he'd need it.

Or maybe the test was simply whether he would take a cookie, no matter what kind.

Or maybe the cookies had been left there by a previous hermit crossing the bridge. Was it possible? The hermit didn't know. Could be.

And then, perhaps, just perhaps, the purpose of the

cookies was simply to get him to think about all this stuff. Just to think. Well, he was doing that, all right. On the other hand, maybe he wasn't supposed to think. Maybe he was supposed to just do something, spur of the moment, and by thinking about it he had already failed the test.

This was the kind of thing the hermit—our hermit, and any other hermit, for that matter—had to deal with. Store owners had shoplifters. Comedians had hecklers. Fry cooks had grease burns.

And hermits had weird stuff happen for no apparent reason when they meditated. But it's just no *apparent* reason. Always, always, somehow, some way, there's a reason for everything.

Ah, to heck with it. The hermit closed his eyes, reached into the bag, and pulled out a cookie. It was oatmeal. He chomped down on it and ate as he continued walking, bag in hand. Yes, he was taking the bag.

Now, the hermit had never been much of a cookie eater, but that was what he was given, so that was what he had. Cookies.

All he needed to do now, as far as he could tell, was figure out who that girl was. He had seen other people, other beings, at other steps along his journey. But they had always belonged there. He didn't really know how he could tell, but there had never been any doubt in his mind. Each person, each being he had encountered, had had some sort of purpose that helped him along the way.

He didn't have that feeling about this girl. It was unsettling.

It was always possible, he supposed, that that was the whole idea behind having her there—to send him into unsettlement. He was pretty sure it wasn't, though.

At least he had cookies. He finished that oatmeal fella and reached into the bag again.

***

The mayor's daughter bit into her oatmeal cookie and chewed slowly. She opened her closet and checked out the clothes, eyeballing each item, evaluating, envisioning, and so on. Tonight was going to be a night out. It was going to be a special night out because it was her first time since the news story on TV. It had caused something of a stir, she knew, and she wasn't sure how people at the tavern would react to her.

At the soup kitchen, and at the animal shelter, people were friendlier. Well, not friendlier so much as a little warmer. Maybe warmer isn't quite the right word. Let's say they were more amiable. Oh, I know: genial. People were more genial.

What she had always had going for her at those places, the soup kitchen and the animal shelter, was that even if people didn't approve of her personal behavior—or, that is to say, her rumored personal behavior, they could at least see she was doing something to help make the world a better place.

You know what? We could say people were friendlier.

So the mayor's daughter looked over her wardrobe. Anything she wore would of course be the height of village fashion. It was just a matter of finding something in keeping with her mood. So she put on her best Duran Duran T-shirt and orange corduroy pants.

What the heck kind of mood was that? I don't pretend to know.

The mayor's daughter breezed into the tavern like a sports star arriving to greet autograph seekers. No one was seeking her autograph, though. She just liked to pretend. (She could, however, play a pretty strong game of tennis on a good day.)

She took her usual place at the bar. The bartender—the mayor's daughter was still keeping him in reserve—was trying to figure her out. Dressed the way she was, she was clearly looking for trouble. But they had said on the TV that she was virtuous. What was going on?

Guys checked her out. They were interested. Of course they were; how could they not be? She checked them out. That was why she was there. And finally she found herself talking to a nice young man who seemed to be someone who could excite her in all the ways she liked to be excited.

"I hear you're wholesome and virtuous," he said.

"That's what the rumor says."

"Are you?"

"Do you want me to be?"

The inane flirting went on for a while longer. (I don't want to write any more of it, and you don't want to read any more of it.) Finally, they decided to go back to his place.

And as you'd expect, there was noise. There was hootin' and hollerin', bangin' and thumpin'. Furniture flew about the room. A small vortex appeared near the ceiling. There were seismic disturbances. Some of the neighbors reported seeing a ghostly vision of Franklin Delano Roosevelt in the sky.

And the guy. Oh, the guy. Nine hours later a policeman found him crawling from the apartment building, semi-conscious and barely lucid, with his clothes in tatters. His legs were painted hunter green. He was taken to the hospital and given an IV to replenish his fluids because he was dangerously close to dehydrating.

When he woke up the next day, the first thing he said was, "I think I'm in love."

A guy in a fedora and a trench coat was lurking just outside the door. As soon as he heard the mayor's daughter's guy say he was in love, he snuck away and made a phone call. He called the opposing party chairman. "She's really not wholesome," the caller reported. "She really gave it to that guy, lucky fella." Yeah, he was the private investigator the opposing party had hired to find out about that awful news report.

"We know what the girl is doing," the chairman said. "You understand you're supposed to be investigating those news stories, don't you?"

"Well, I'm just getting started," the private investigator said, abashed. He had no idea what he was going to do with all those photographs he had taken.

***

And the hermit continued on his way across the Bridge of Constant Focus. The sky was a lovely, deep orange. At one point he thought he noticed a small vortex off to one side, but it didn't seem to matter.

***

Two weeks went by. The mayor's political party planted

a couple more stories in the TV news, providing more details. The first story was about an interview they claimed to have conducted with the mayor's daughter. She didn't want to appear on camera, they said, but she wanted the village to know that she was very upset with the bad rumors about her behavior. She was grateful that the TV news was giving her a chance to tell her side of the story. (It might be noted that attentive TV viewers came away from the show thinking that although the segment had included a lot of highly emotional stuff about the girl's reputation, it had very little—well, nothing, in fact—in the way of actually telling her side of the story.)

The second planted story said that one of the guys who had spread the shocking rumors had been a known troublemaker and ne'er-do-well in the town he lived in before this one. Another one of the guys, the story said, claimed to communicate with the ghost of Dolly Madison on a regular basis. Yeah, how much credibility did *that* guy have, eh?

Yet the news stories, clever and devious though they were, were offset by the mayor's daughter's behavior. She wasn't stopping her escapades. And it seemed the rumors about those escapades were taking on more credibility as they continued to spread around the village. A particularly bad version of one of the rumors included a variety of extraterrestrial creatures as an audience. For some reason, the creatures were explicitly identified as electricians, truck drivers, art teachers, web site designers, printing press operators, and flute teachers.

The chairman of the mayor's political party was not pleased. The mayor was supposed to be reining his daughter in, and apparently a big cloud of failure was hanging over whatever attempts he might have made, if any.

The chairman went to the mayor's office to have a little talk.

"We need to have a talk," he said.

The mayor paused the Punch-O-Rama boxing game he was playing on his computer. Three-Armed Thurston was frozen in mid-punch. "What's on your mind?" the mayor asked.

"Do you know your daughter is still cavorting with the young men of the village?"

"Well, that's nice," the mayor said.

The chairman stared at him for a moment. "Uh, do you know what cavorting means?"

He didn't. He made up something on the spot. "Doesn't it have something to do with picking up litter?"

"No, that's not what it means. It means she's still picking up guys and going home with them and engaging in shocking and immoral behavior."

"That's a lot of activity for one little word."

"Don't worry about the word," the chairman said. "The point is, you have to control that girl. We can't have her doing stuff like that."

The mayor sighed. "I understand," he said.

"Do you understand how important it is?"

"Yes, we've talked about this before. She could lose the next election for us. Believe me, I understand. I don't want to end up unemployed."

The chairman sat back and regarded the mayor. "Can you find some way to control her?"

"I think so." Actually, the mayor had absolutely no

idea what he might do to control his daughter, but he was pretty sure the chairman wanted to hear a "yes." The mayor aimed to please. It was how he had gotten to be mayor.

"Good. I would prefer it if you could handle her on your own. But if the problem continues much longer, we might have to step in with drastic measures."

This scared the mayor. It conjured up images in his mind of someone being stuffed into a fifty-five-gallon drum and left in a landfill. That would suck. Places like that stink, and there's nothing good to eat. "I promise you won't have to do that," the mayor said.

In reality, the chairman had no intention of harming anyone. The more drastic measure he had in mind was simply to have the party run a different candidate next time. But the mayor didn't have to know that. The chairman figured the uncertainty would give the mayor greater incentive to keep the girl in line.

***

So that night, the mayor had another talk with his daughter. He didn't want to tell her about the chairman's threat of drastic measures because he didn't want to scare her. Besides, he wasn't sure which one of them would end up in the fifty-five-gallon drum.

"Daughter, I've heard more stories that you've been misbehaving."

"You can't believe everything you hear, daddy. I mean, my goodness. You know how they blamed me when those stars collided in the Andromeda galaxy? It was, like, SO totally not my fault."

"The problem, sweetheart, isn't that you cause a lot

of disturbances with...uh...your activity. The problem is just that your behavior is so disgraceful."

"You think I'm disgraceful?"

"No, sweetheart. No, no, no, not at all." My goodness, he thought. How could I have handled it so badly? (But he didn't handle it all that badly. It's just that she was just handling him very well.) "No, you're not disgraceful at all."

"Oh, thank you, daddy." She lunged forward and gave him a great big ol' hug around the neck and a kiss on the cheek. "You're the best daddy *ever*." And with that, the mayor's daughter turned and bounded out like an excited kangaroo.

A half hour later he was still sitting motionless, trying to think of a reply.

***

The hermit continued his journey along the Bridge of Constant Focus. As he walked, he enjoyed the day. The sun was bright, the air was fresh, and birds were chirping. The bridge spanned a river of chicken noodle soup, which gave off a nice, wholesome aroma. And he had his bag of cookies.

All was right in the world of meditation and spirituality.

The hermit thought about things. He thought about movies, some of the films he had seen before he started hermit school. He thought about *It's a Wonderful Life* and *Manhattan*.

He had a spring in his step.

CHAPTER FOUR

Meanwhile, the mayor's daughter was busy trying to turn some poor sap inside out, metaphorically speaking. He was someone she'd played with before, so he knew what he was in for, and she was familiar with the material she had to work with.

It was the usual flurry of intense activity the village had come to expect. There was the usual roar that sounded like a steel mill in full production (along with the accompanying heat), the seismic disturbances, the confused animals within a five-mile radius, and the intermittent disruptions in over-the-air television signals.

By now, the hospital had learned that phenomena like these meant they should be ready for a new patient coming to the emergency room. They should be ready for a guy who was delirious, suffering from exhaustion, and dehydrated. They should get a room ready so they could keep him under observation for the next forty-eight to seventy-two hours. He would be okay if he was taken care of properly.

And sure enough, the poor sap was found crawling along the roadside just outside of town, delirious and feverish, and with bruises covering eighty percent of his body. His clothing was torn and his hair had been, for some reason, colored purple and yellow in a tasteful paisley pattern. As soon as they got him stabilized in the ER, he was heard to say what so many of these young men were heard to say: “I think I’m in love.”

Make of that what you will.

The mayor’s daughter snuck back home, climbed in through her bedroom window, and pretended nothing had happened. She slipped into bed just as her daddy, the mayor, knocked on her door.

“Yes, daddy?”

“Just checking,” he said. “Is everything okay?” He had noticed the disturbances. Who wouldn’t have?

“Everything’s okay, daddy,” she said, and snuggled up more cozy into her blankets. “Everything.”

“Okay, sweetie.”

That was good enough for him. He let himself be convinced that she had been there all along.

***

And the hermit? Well, it turned out that the Bridge of Constant Focus was actually a drawbridge. Halfway across, the road ahead of him suddenly turned upward, leading to the heavens. Well, that was what he thought at first. In reality, the drawbridge was open. He couldn’t go any farther until someone lowered it.

He looked around for a button or a lever or some kind of mechanism. He couldn’t find anything. He leaned out over the railing and could see the motor that moved the movable part. Unfortunately, he couldn’t see any wires or conduits leading from the motor. If he could see the wires, he could follow them and find the controls.

Apparently it operated on a wireless signal. There was a thing sticking out that looked like an antenna. That meant the controls could be anywhere. If he had lived years ago, before people were zinging wireless signals through the air, he would have seen wires.

Daggone it! (Okay, I know. You're probably thinking that it needed wiring for electricity. I say you're thinking too much.)

Had he passed anything along the way that might be a control? There must be a booth for an operator to sit in, he thought. Something like that should be easy to see. He was sure he hadn't seen a booth. Well, pretty sure. Sure enough that he was pretty well opposed to turning around and going back to look for one. It was entirely possible that this thing was operated by someone who pushed a button on a console located deep down in the seventh sub-basement of a building somewhere in a huge city hundreds of miles distant.

No way was he going to find something like that.

But just to make sure, he decided to suck it up and backtrack. He walked back the way he had come, slowly, looking around very carefully and trying to think about everything he was seeing. The control could be disguised as something else. Anything, anything at all could be the switch that would lower the bridge.

The hermit walked for miles and miles. The open part of the bridge receded out of sight. He reached the table where he had found the cookies. He examined it. He turned it upside down and studied the bottom. He pushed and pulled on the legs to see whether they would move somehow. After hours of close study, he decided it was nothing but a solid wood table.

He still had a long way to go, just to backtrack. He

couldn't see the open part sticking up, and he couldn't see the shore. This sucked.

There was nothing to do but keep going back. He continued for a couple more days, careful to notice everything around him, looking for clues. He had the bag of cookies, and he was careful to ration them out to make them last as long as possible. No, he didn't have to eat in his meditative state. He wouldn't starve to death, no matter what. But still, he could feel hunger if he stayed there long enough. And, by golly, those cookies were delicious.

Finally, the hermit reached the beginning of the bridge. He looked around and looked around again. Nothing on the bridge was out of the ordinary. The shoreline was featureless.

The drawbridge had no controls. He was sure of it.

The hermit wanted a nap. He stepped away from the road leading to the bridge so he wouldn't get run over if someone drove a truck through—not likely in a meditative state, but you never know—and lay down.

He dreamed of tidal waves and earthquakes and tornadoes and other major weather disturbances and natural disasters. He dreamed of fires and floods. He dreamed of trains chugging into tunnels.

He awoke, no longer sleepy but not at all refreshed.

Still, tired or not, the only thing he could think of was to go back to where the drawbridge was open. It might have gone back down. It might go back down for some reason later. He didn't know.

So the hermit trudged on, past the upended cookie table, on to the upended drawbridge. And yes, it was still up.

He sat down on the roadway and ate a sugar cookie.

The chicken noodle soup flowing under the bridge sure smelled good, but he had no way to get any.

***

Back at the village, the mayor's political party was holding another secret meeting. Secret, that is, as far as the mayor was concerned. All the other party officials knew about it, and they were there.

The chairman summed up the problem: "We have this big, fancy New York public relations firm planting stories in the news to counteract the scandal of the mayor's daughter. We have a lot of people in the village believing that these rumors of her behavior are actually a smear campaign being carried out by the opposing party."

"Sweet," one of the other party officials said.

"Yes," the chairman said. "Very sweet, except for one thing. The mayor isn't holding up his end of the plan. He's supposed to make sure the girl behaves, and she's just going merrily on, playing with the young men of the village. When people see that she really is doing all this scandalous stuff, that the rumors are true (even if they're exaggerated), nothing we plant in the news is going to help us."

There was a loud murmur of concern among the meeting attendees.

"The big problem is that the mayor was supposed to control the girl, and he's not doing it. It's as if he's wallowing around in a big pool of failure."

There was a loud murmur of agreement among the meeting attendees.

"So," the chairman continued, "The way I see it, we

need to take matters into our own hands."

"How do we do that?" someone asked.

"We can spread a rumor that she has a bunch of awful diseases. Then no one will want to play with her."

"Let me get this straight," the chairman said. "You seem to think it's better that we have a rumor that she's promiscuous and disease ridden than a rumor that she's just promiscuous."

"Oh, well, I hadn't thought of it like that."

"Any other suggestions?"

"Maybe we could just arrange for her to...disappear," someone else suggested.

"What kind of rumors to you think we'd have to deal with then?"

"Uh, ones that are not good?"

"Yes, ones that are not good." Sometimes the chairman of the party wondered how anything ever got done in the village, considering the caliber of leadership he saw.

"What if she got married?" someone asked.

Hmmm...The chairman would have to think about that one. They wouldn't have to get her married, but maybe if she were to meet a really cool guy she really, really liked, she might decide to stick with him for a while. They didn't need her to be celibate; being monogamous would be good enough.

But it would have to be a very special guy. Not some ordinary schmuck who just happened to be cute. Not your everyday, average Joe who was a steady guy, who was thought of by the mothers of daughters as a "good catch." No, a guy like that wouldn't be good enough. They needed someone super-special.

So the party put on a big, huge, highly secret search

for just the right guy. He would have to be tall and good-looking, very manly and virile and muscular. He'd have to have a lot of endurance.

They sent guys out to all the big cities to search. They sent guys to New York and Chicago and Dallas. They sent a guy to Wonder Lick, South Dakota because they'd heard a story about some guy there, but it didn't pan out. The guy they'd heard about, he turned out to be eighty-four years old. Although he had been quite something many years ago, back in the day, he was just kind of old and wrinkled up now. Their information was out of date.

They sent guys to Kansas City. They sent guys to Miami. They sent guys to Los Angeles.

They found a guy. I'm not going to say where, but they found a guy. He was tall and manly. He was all the adjectives the mayor's party was looking for. He had a deep, booming voice, and he was fierce and proud. When he stood still, he looked like a statue in a public park.

It took some wheeling and dealing to get him to come to the village. They told him all about their problem, about the mayor's daughter. They showed him pictures of her and repeated all the rumors, including the seismic disturbances and such.

The tall, manly guy was interested. He had been looking for a woman who could be his equal, someone who could keep up with his various and voracious appetites and appreciate the things he considered the finer things in life.

This mayor's daughter person...she sounded intriguing. Yes, indeed.

The tall, manly guy didn't have any doubt that he

could win her heart. I mean, come on! He had it all, the complete package! He could steal the freakin' first lady away from the freakin' president if he wanted! (Don't worry. He doesn't want to.)

"Yes, I can do it," he told them. "I can make her fall in love with me and forget about having anything to do with anyone else."

"Are you sure?" they asked. "This girl...she's a force of nature."

But that only increased his interest. "So am I, my friend. So am I."

Yes, the tall, manly guy was willing to talk about it. He was interested—very interested—but he played it cool. *They* had approached *him*, after all, and he continued to let them think they needed him more than he needed them. He wasn't going to come cheap.

"Here's the deal," the tall, manly guy said. "I'll need a job in the village."

"No problem."

"I'll need one of those jobs where you get paid a whole lot but don't have do to anything or show up at the office. Can you fix it up for me?"

"Hey, we have a job just like that waiting for you already. A choice of two, actually. Would you like a job with a private company or a job with the government?"

"Which has better benefits?"

"You can look over the information and decide which one you like better."

"Okay, and I'll need a car."

"No problem."

"And a house."

"We have one all ready for you."

"A big one, furnished?"

"Of course. I'm insulted that you'd even ask."

"I'll also need a popcorn popper, the collected works of Charles Bukowski, a wood lathe, five to ten spider plants, a set of cookie cutters shaped like astrological signs, a hood ornament from a 1953 Nash Metropolitan, and an antique Bakelite figurine of Andrew Jackson."

"Wait a minute." The village search contingent with drew to a back corner of the room to confer. Blah, blah, blah. They came back to the tall, manly guy. "We can get all that stuff," the leader of the group said. "But we might have to get the hood ornament from a '52 Nash Metropolitan."

"Well, I dunno," the tall, manly guy said. "It's kinda important that it's from a '53." Actually, it wasn't. He didn't need the hood ornament at all, from any car. He was making demands just because he could.

"I think we can find a '53 if you give us a little extra time." That's what the leader of the search contingent said, but in reality he was just going to give the tall, manly guy whatever they could find and tell him it was a '53. He was sure the tall, manly guy would never know the difference.

"Yeah, sure," the tall, manly guy said. He was pretty sure the officials from the village were just going to give him whatever they could find and tell him it was a 1953 model, counting on him not to know the difference. He was also pretty sure they were going to do something similar with the Bakelite figurine. He didn't care. He just wanted to make them look for something to give him.

So the deal was struck. It would take a couple weeks to make all the arrangements for the tall, manly guy to move to the village. They just had to hope that in the meantime, the mayor's daughter wouldn't do anything too outrageous.

***

At the Bridge of Constant Focus, the hermit sat at the raised portion of the drawbridge, waiting for it to go down, hungry for chicken noodle soup. He could eat only so many cookies, and the wholesome aroma of the soup passing under the bridge was getting stronger. He was getting hungrier. He could imagine himself with a mouthful of the delicious soup, savoring the goodness, and then swallowing. He felt, or imagined he could feel, the soup easing down his throat into his stomach, filling him with a sense of well-being. He imagined the nutritious nutrients from the food spreading through his body.

As it was, he felt kinda nauseated after eating nothing but cookies for the last few days. In the meditative world, that is. Sometimes the distinction blurs, especially when you get to the advanced steps.

He was nauseated enough to realize he couldn't stay there any longer, sitting around waiting for something to happen. He had an idea. It was a crazy idea, but it was one of those ideas that were crazy enough that they just might work.

The hermit stood and picked up his bag of cookies. He didn't relish the thought of eating more of them, but they were all he had—for the time being, anyway.

Once again, he walked back the way he had come. Eventually, he came to the table, just where he had left it, upside-down with the legs sticking up, looking like some sort of postmodern sculpture of a cat lying on its back.

The hermit studied the table. He walked around it to get a view of it from all angles. He looked over the edge of the bridge and checked out the chicken noodle soup flowing so deliciously below.

He put the cookies down, very deliberately, as if it were part of a ritual. He stepped onto the underside of the tabletop. He grasped one of the table legs with both hands and gave it a little tug, just as a test. It was firm.

The hermit put his all into it. He pulled back and then jerked forward, trying to break the leg off. He worked and worked at it, and after a few minutes he heard a nice cracking sound. He worked at it some more and was able to get the leg off completely.

It took about forty-five minutes to break off all four legs. The hermit stood back and regarded his work. Yes, that looked good. Now all he had to do was hope this thing would float.

He dragged the tabletop over to the edge of the bridge, on the side where the soup was flowing toward him. He hefted the tabletop up onto the railing and then flung it off as far as he could into the distance. He watched as it caught the air like a Frisbee and flew for several thrilling seconds, going about twenty yards out. Now, you might think an old man couldn't heave a tabletop that far—or, for that matter, any distance at all—but remember, this is the meditative world, and they play by a different set of rules. You have to be very alert at all times in the meditative world. You have to *think*. So anyway, he watched it sail through the air—the tabletop, that is—and hit the water. It made a bit ol' splash, and then it sank...

...and so did the hermit's heart. He had really hoped this would work. No matter, he told himself. If it wasn't going to float, he had no use for it anyway.

And then he saw it bob back up to the surface. It was just the momentum of falling that had carried it underwater—or, that is to say, undersoup—initially, but there it was: it was floating!

It slowly drifted back toward the bridge. The hermit watched for a moment, gauging the tabletop's speed and distance, calculating in his head.

In the physical world, he would have been too old for this kind of thing. In the meditative world, he thought he could probably do it. He'd have to try, anyway.

As the tabletop disappeared under the bridge, the hermit rushed across to the other side, climbed over the rail, and dove in. It was a perfect dive; he cut through the soup beautifully just about three feet away from the tabletop. He kicked back up to the surface, opened his eyes, and looked around.

Yes, there it was, the tabletop. He swam over and climbed on.

As he had hoped, it was buoyant enough to support his weight. He sat cross-legged on his raft—his tabletop repurposed as a raft—and looked up at the bridge. Dang, it was high. He had no idea he had dived so far.

The hermit scooped up several handfuls of soup with his hands. It tasted every bit as good as it smelled. This was the real deal, like mom used to make at home, with her own two hands—not that oversalted stuff they sell in cans. No, this had big, thick noodles and hefty chunks of chicken meat, and carrots and celery and stuff.

He ate as much soup as he could and then took the

bag of cookies out of his shirt pocket. Sadly—or maybe not so sadly, since he was tired of them—the cookies were soaked through and through with chicken soup broth. He laid the bag down on the raft and began paddling with his hands.

***

Moving day came for the tall, manly guy, and he saw his new house for the first time. He was pleased. It was all fresh and painted, fitted out with new and fashionable furniture, with phone service already working and the running water ready to run. It had a well-equipped, modern, state-of-the-art gym so he could keep his manly physique in its peak condition—and you know the equipment had to be good because it had cool-looking electronic displays that flashed numbers and stuff all the time.

All he had to do was walk in the front door, turn on the television set, and sit down. Then he would be living there. Even if it was raining, he wouldn't care.

As he sank ever deeper into his recliner, watching TV, the party officials crowded around him. "Well," they asked, "Do you like it?"

"It'll do," he said. Actually, it was much nicer than he had hoped for, but he was playing it cool. "What about my job?"

"We have it all fixed up. We've even opened a bank account for you, with a deposit to start you out. Think of it as a signing bonus. We think you'll find it very generous." The party chairman handed the tall, manly guy a bank book. He took it and looked, prepared to not be impressed. It was indeed quite a large sum.

"Yes," the tall, manly guy said. "This is very generous. Thank you."

"Nothing's too good for the man who's going to solve our biggest problem."

The tall, manly guy slipped the bank book into his shirt pocket and picked up the remote. "I'll get started on our little project tomorrow," he said. "For now, I'd like you guys to clear out of here so I can watch a little *Green Acres* and get settled in."

Across the street, the private investigator was hiding behind a tree. He whipped out his cell phone and called the opposing party chairman. "The tall, manly guy just moved into his new house," he said.

"What does that have to do with the news stories about us?" the chairman asked.

Gosh. "Well, uh…I haven't figured that out yet," the investigator said, mainly because he knew he had better not say "nothing."

***

They didn't throw the tall, manly guy together with the mayor's daughter right away. Oh, no. This wasn't going to be some lame, half-baked, cockamamie scheme they were going to carelessly dive into. They had to do some preparation first. They had already gone to considerable expense just to get this guy into the village, and they wanted to make sure they did everything right.

Operatives for the mayor's political party had made a detailed study of the mayor's daughter's taste in men. They researched what guys had been wearing when she picked them up. They researched hairstyles. They researched stuff she was interested in. They left nothing to chance.

They fitted the tall, manly guy out with a carefully selected wardrobe, all in the height of village fashion, and all in colors chosen to appeal to the mayor's daughter. They took him to a hair salon. They coached him in subjects the mayor's daughter was interested in, things like Halley's Comet, the works of F. Scott Fitzgerald, the influence of *The Art of War* on biochemical research, and more.

The preparations took about a month. In the meantime, there were more guys—for the mayor's daughter, that is—and more noise that sounded as if the moon had crashed into the Earth just over there on the other side of the mountain, more weather incidents, and so on. One person reported seeing what he described as a "minor demon" sitting calmly on a crate and smoking a pipe in a vacant lot when one of the encounters was known to take place. But as it was generally believed that minor demons could be contained only by means mastered by the highest spiritual adepts, and since the minor demon was never seen again, the report was generally discounted.

Except by the rumor spreaders, of course. One version of the story had a band of thirteen major demons roaming the streets incinerating small animals by pointing at them and insatiably having their way with any unfortunate people who happened to be around.

The party officials hoped the tall, manly guy would be ready to start working on his assignment soon.

And he was. The party arranged for him to get a job at the animal shelter where the mayor's daughter worked. The owners of the shelter were in on the scheme. They weren't going to fire her for her scandalous behavior, but they'd be happy if someone could get her to stop. And all they had to do was give up some unused office space for a while.

Now, mind you, this wasn't the job the tall, manly guy had asked for, where he wouldn't have to show up or do anything and still get paid a lot of money. That was all fixed up and going well. This was a different job where he didn't have to do anything, but he had to show up so he could get close to the mayor's daughter.

They set him up in an office down at the end of the hallway, complete with his name on the door.He had a desk and a computer and a phone.

He would come in about nine thirty in the morning, dressed sharply and carrying a briefcase. He'd greet the receptionist with a tone that implied he had some actual authority around the place and stride purposefully down the hallway to his office. He'd spend the morning on the Internet, arguing on message boards, and when it was the mayor's daughter's lunchtime he'd go to the employee break room to be there with her.

It was very important, they had told him, not to come on too strong. Her modus operandi was that she always made the first move, and they wanted to let her do that this time. The plan was that she would latch onto him, and when she saw that he could withstand—with aplomb—the rigorous demands of satisfying the excessive desires of her voracious appetites and come back for more—and not only that, but talk to her about stuff she was interested in—she would be hooked.

So they hoped.

The tall, manly guy sauntered into the break room the first day with *The Art of War* under his arm. He whistled nonchalantly, acting casual, not too terribly concerned about anything that might be going on around him.

He got a drink from the soda machine and sat down with the lunch he had brought, a self-heating serving of chicken noodle soup. It was the kind like mom used to make, with big, thick noodles and hefty chunks of chicken meat, and carrots and celery and stuff. It was good.

So he sat at his table eating and reading, holding the book up so that anyone who came in would see what he was reading. A couple minutes later, the mayor's daughter came in. She took her lunch out of the refrigerator, popped it into the microwave, and stood there looking around as she waited.

And she saw the tall, manly guy reading *The Art of War*. Interesting, she thought. After the microwave said "ding," she took her lunch and went over to his table. "Can I sit with you?" she asked.

"Well, I guess so," he said. "I was reading, but I can read at home." They had told him to act shy.

The mayor's daughter sat down. "I see you're reading *The Art of War*," she said. "I'm interested in that, especially the way it has influenced biochemical research."

The tall, manly guy put the book down. "Yes, fascinating subject," he said. "I particularly admire Rimbaud and Perseid's work in the field."

"Oh, yes. They did groundbreaking research at Betrug Polytechnic Institute."

"And the paper they published in the Onzin Annals of Science. Oh, to die for!"

They talked for a while, with the tall, manly guy regurgitating stuff he'd memorized but didn't really understand. The mayor's daughter didn't make any overt moves on him, not in *that* way, but she was intrigued.

***

Meanwhile, the hermit noticed that the current in the chicken soup was shifting and taking him toward the far shore. Why? He didn't know, and he didn't care. The main thing was, it meant he could stop paddling. He could just sit there and enjoy the ride and scoop up some soup whenever he got hungry. Life was sweet.

He rode his raft to the shore and landed about a hundred yards from the bridge.

He had gotten past the Bridge of Constant Focus.

CHAPTER FIVE

The mayor had heard more rumors from time to time, but since the chairman of the party hadn't yelled at him or demanded he do something, he wasn't going to sweat it.

And the chairman? He sat in his office and listened to the tall, manly guy give his report. "We talked for a while," the tall, manly guy said.

"Good, good."

"We talked for a while, and we were both late coming back from our lunch break."

"Late? Because of talking? Good, good."

"Well, it didn't matter for me. Her supervisor wasn't happy about it."

"She'll get over it. Did the mayor's daughter let on that she wanted to commit sexual atrocities with you?"

"No. She was very friendly, though. I think she's interested."

"Good, good."

And so the plan proceeded. The tall, manly guy and the mayor's daughter had lunch together every day for the whole week. They talked about stuff. And finally, she went for it. "Would you like to take me home?" she asked.

"Home?" He pretended he didn't understand, as if he had no idea what they would do there.

"Yes, home. We can..." She paused and looked around to make sure no one was within earshot. "We can take off all our clothes and do things."

"Oh, really?"

"Yes, really. Lots of pleasurable things. Over and over and over again."

"Well, I like pleasure," the tall, manly guy said.

"I'm sure you do. It's so...pleasurable. And I think you're the type of man who could really appreciate things like that."

"Oh, yes, no doubt."

"So, can I come over tonight?"

"Well, yeah, sure. If you want."

"I want."

Back in his office, the tall, manly guy called the party chairman. "She asked to come over to my house tonight."

"Good, good."

"She wants to do pleasurable things."

"Good, good."

***

After work, the mayor's daughter called her best friend. "I'm going over to his house tonight," she said.

"You're going to do the usual?"

"Well, of course. But there's more to it. We've been talking."

"Talking?"

"Yes. He and I have been talking. Not only is he a marvelous specimen of tall, manly manhood, but he likes a lot of the things I like. We've talked about Halley's Comet, the works of F. Scott Fitzgerald, the influence of *The Art of War* on biochemical research, and lots of other stuff."

"You mean..."

"Yes, exactly, best friend. We have things in common and he's, like, interesting and stuff."

"That's great!"

"Yeah. It kinda seemed he repeated himself on a lot of the ideas we talked about, like he would say something, and then the next day he'd say exactly the same thing again, repeated himself in exactly the same words. If I didn't know better, I might think he just memorized the material just to impress me and didn't really know what he was talking about."

"Oh?"

"Well, yeah, but then, why on earth would anyone do that?"

"I can't imagine."

"Me neither. The main thing is I'm going to misbehave tonight in a most delightful way."

The mayor's daughter wanted to make a good impression, so she spent extra time getting fixed up especially nice. She wanted him to see that she had made an effort.

Holy smoke! She realized that maybe she actually liked this tall, manly guy!

Well, she thought, we'll just see how it goes.

The two of them had dinner. They ate some food and listened to a little music and talked about the things they liked to talk about. Or, rather, the things she liked to talk about. The tall, manly guy was still on automatic pilot with the conversational stuff. It bugged the mayor's daughter just a little bit, back in the back of her mind, but she was trying her best to give him the benefit of the doubt. That he seemed to be shy made it easier for her to do that.

Besides, conversation wasn't the main item on the agenda for the evening.

The mayor's daughter finally decided that it was time to get down to business and address the main item on the agenda. The tall, manly guy continued the shy act, but he was agreeable.

So they got down to business, and it was monumental. There were noises like whales mating at a Ted Nugent concert. There were tremors and shakings that made people think the village was under attack with weapons not yet invented. A statue in the village square fell over. A small bridge over a stream in the middle of town collapsed.

And the mayor's daughter and the tall, manly guy were sated—nine hours later. It should also be noted that he wasn't found wandering around delirious somewhere on the other side of the village. He was there in his own bed, in relatively good condition (physically and mentally), next to the mayor's daughter.

Both called in sick at the animal shelter the next day. Of course, it didn't matter for the tall, manly guy because he didn't do anything anyway. As far as the mayor's daughter was concerned, the boss was willing to let it slide because in spite of the mayor's daughter's attempts to make her voice sound raspy and give a few fake coughs during the call so she would sound sick, she (the boss) knew exactly what had happened and why. The boss was willing to let it slide because, of course, she was in on this little plan to get the mayor's daughter to fall in love, and if this was what it took, it would be worth it in the long run.

The happy couple spent most of the next day unconscious, and then they woke up and started all over again. The tall, manly guy was very well up to the task, and he was happy to do it. In fact, he kept thinking, "Gee whiz, this is my freakin' *job*! How sweet is that?"

***

The chairman of the mayor's political party called the fancy New York PR firm. "Things are going well with the mayor's daughter," he said. "We've figured out a way to get her to fall in love with this tall, manly guy we found. I think she'll be happy with him for a while."

"Good," said the partner who was working on the campaign.

"So we think she's under control for a while. I don't think she'll do anything to undermine any more of the stories you guys plant in the news."

"Excellent."

***

Up on the mountainside, the hermit was celebrating his completion of the Bridge of Constant Focus. He poured a bit of homemade carrot wine into his homemade cup, which he had made at home out of leaves he had woven together. At hermit school they had taught him how to carve things out of wood, things like bowls and plates and cups, and they had also taught him pottery, so he might be able to make tableware. But he wasn't good at any of that stuff. The best he could manage was to weave leaves together to make those things. Even at that his cups were leaky, so he had to pour and drink quickly. The upside was that he found it was a real good way to drink his carrot wine. (It must be noted that no one is too spiritually advanced to enjoy a little nip now and then.)

He poured and drank, and wine dribbled down his chin and onto his shirt. He had expected that; what he hadn't expected was the amount of wine that dribbled. Well, that happened, too. Eventually his cups and plates and bowls would get soggy and leaky, and he would have to make new ones. So it was time for a new cup. He hadn't had this one very long, though. No matter. Leaves were free and easy to get. He was in the middle of a freakin' forest, for Pete's sake, which was like a huge leaf factory. Except that it wasn't inside a big, drafty, noisy building with a concrete floor.

But now wasn't the time for making cups just yet. Now was the time for celebrating. He would just have to pour and drink even faster.

Yeah, no problem.

***

About that time, another e-mail made its way from the fake fancy New York PR firm to the TV station:

> As you know, details about our devious and evil plot to discredit the mayor have come out on the TV news. How, oh how, could we have been so careless? You can rest assured that we're investigating to find out who's been leaking information.
> We've been holding meetings, and of course if we've

> been holding meetings that tells you how seriously we take this matter.
>
> While we do that, we're moving forward with Stage Two of the evil and devious plan. Even though the things we have already done have been made public, we don't think there's anything they can do to stop Stage Two. HA HA HA HA HA HA HA!!!!!!!

Yes, they talked about the sinister-sounding Stage Two. It was the oldest trick in the book: The Unspecified Threat. It was apparently big and unstoppable, something that was indeed worth the waste of much time to worry about.

Once again, the town was abuzz. What was going on? they wondered. Was the opposing party plotting a coup? The uncertainty was agonizing.

And officials of the opposing party were apoplectic. "We have to stop this!" the opposing party chairman shouted at a meeting—yes, they were holding a meeting, which shows how seriously they were taking the matter. "We know these e-mails they're reading on the news are fake. We know it, but the village doesn't. People in the village think it must be true. They think the TV station couldn't put it on the air if it weren't true!"

Indeed. It wasn't comfortable for opposing party officials. People didn't trust them. People looked at them askance on the street. Mothers shielded their children's eyes when they saw the officials in public. Or if they didn't do that, they would point to the officials and say, "Look, there. Look at that man. He's a bad man. Don't grow up to be like him. He's bad."

The kid would stand there, blinking blankly, not knowing what the heck mommy (or daddy) was talking about. Still, it was uncomfortable for all concerned.

The chairman pointed at the private investigator, who was staring at a poster of Richard Brautigan that happened to be mounted on the wall. "What have you done?" the chairman screamed at him.

The investigator started. "Uh, well, uh..." he said, "I think we should get to the bottom of all this."

"Yes! That's the whole idea! What are you going to do?"

It filtered through to the investigator's awareness for the first time that they actually expected him to do something. What a bummer. "I should get in touch with the company that's sending these e-mails to the TV station."

"Yes!" everyone shouted. It was deafening, a feat all the more impressive considering only five people were there.

"It's decided, then," the chairman said. "The private investigator will contact this company and see what the heck is going on." And he banged his gavel.

***

The next morning the temp worker at the fake PR firm was sitting at her desk in the basement of the abandoned warehouse. It was lonely down there, dreary and chilly and not very well lit. All she had to do was this: Every few days an e-mail would come in, and she would forward it to some little TV station located in a little village she'd never heard of. She didn't understand why. All she understood was that the people who were paying her wanted her to sit there and do that, and also answer the phone if it happened to ring so as to convince the caller that this was a functional office, and that was all she needed to understand.

Good enough. It was better than one of those jobs where you go home with grease burns. Except that it was lonely. And kinda spooky. And chilly.

So the temp was reading *The Tao of Pooh* when the phone rang for the very first time. Now, mind you, she had been there for several weeks, and this was the first time the phone had rung. The basement was large and empty, with a concrete floor and a high ceiling, so the ringing echoed and reverberated around the room so much she thought for an instant that she was at Pink Floyd concert.

In fact, the temp was about to get out her cigarette lighter so she could fire it up and wave it around when she realized it was the phone.

Oh yeah, the phone. It turned out to be some guy asking whether this was a fancy New York PR firm.

"Yes, sir," she said, as she had carefully been instructed.

"I'd like to speak to someone in charge, please," the man said.

"I'll see whether our junior partner is in. Just a moment, please." She punched a button to switch over to another line and called the real New York PR firm. "This is the temp at the fake PR firm," she said. "I have someone on the other line who wants to talk to someone in charge. I told him I'd see whether our junior partner is in, just like I was told to do."

"I'm sorry, you have the wrong number," a raspy, out-of-breath-sounding voice said. In the background, the temp heard something that sounded like the crack of a whip. Then there was the sound of a car crashing, followed by a donkey braying. The person who answered the phone coughed. "Hey, listen," the raspy voice said, "I gotta get back to…uh, what I was doing…" In the background, a barbershop quartet scat-sang the "Jumping Jack Flash" riff, with a jackhammer as percussion. Then a loud, operatic voice rang out: "I WANT MY TOOTHPASTE!" The raspy voice came back. "Come on over later, if you want to."

"Yeah, sure." The temp hung up and dialed again. This time she got the right number. The receptionist at the big, fancy New York PR firm put her through to one of the many, many junior partners, and they got it fixed up so the junior partner was connected up with the investigator.

The temp hung up her phone and sat back, pleased with herself. This was the most work she had done in one day since she had been there. It was exhilarating. She thought about asking for a raise.

***

"I understand that someone at your firm has leaked e-mails that implicate a certain political party in some kind of devious, evil, nefarious plot against our mayor," the investigator said.

"Well, no. I mean, what gave you that idea?" the junior partner asked.

"That's what the story said when they put it on the news."

"I'm sorry they did that, but we're not responsible for what someone says on a TV news show."

That was true, of course, but there was something about it—the way the junior partner said it, maybe—

that just didn't sound quite right.

It nagged at the investigator. It nagged at him the rest of the day and through the night. He finally decided that the only way he was going to get a satisfactory answer was to go to New York and look this guy square in the eye and talk to him face to face. The thought of going to New York City gave the investigator the heebie-jeebies, but the opposing party officials had made it clear they expected results.

He pulled his suitcase out from under his bed, threw some clothes in, and was on a flight to New York City two hours later.

***

The hermit was at step 137. He didn't know what it was called just yet. After going into his meditative state, he found himself in a parking lot, a vast parking lot stretching out as far as he could see in all directions. All he could see was the pavement and the painted lines and the light posts. Nothing but that, all the way to the horizon, no matter which way he turned.

He would have to start walking. He took the lack of any clues whatsoever as an indication that it didn't matter which way he went.

So he went. And eventually he saw a building looming off in the distance.

***

"So, like, are you in love?"

"If I'm not, it's the next thing to it."

"Oh, how exciting!" The mayor's daughter's best

friend was all atwitter. She was happy, not only because her friend the mayor's daughter had found a really neat guy, but also because the really neat guy might be just the thing to...uh, tone down her antics. Maybe she'd settle down and stick with this guy for a while. The mayor's political party hadn't asked her to help with their plan, but if they had, she would have been thrilled to be part of it.

"I've gone over to his house for the last three nights," the mayor's daughter continued. "And he's just so, so... so tall and manly."

"That's wonderful. I'm so happy for you!"

"Oh, and *so* long lasting!" He was, in fact, because he had undergone intensive training for this assignment and was taking a series of special hormone injections. The mayor's party was leaving nothing to chance.

***

In New York, the investigator had looked up the address of the phony (although he didn't yet know it was phony) fancy New York PR firm and was now in a cab speeding to the address. When the driver stopped at an abandoned warehouse in an old industrial area, the investigator thought something must be wrong. "Are you sure this is the right address?" he asked.

"Yes, sir." The driver pointed to a sign on the front of the building. The address was right on the front of the building in plain letters and numbers, big and bold as if the building were part of a *Sesame Street* set. No one could possibly mistake the huge 137 above the door.

"I don't think this is the place I want," the investigator said. "I'm going to go in, just to make sure, though.

Wait out here, and I'll be back out shortly."

"Yes, sir."

The investigator cautiously approached the warehouse. The whole area had the feel of a bad neighborhood, although he had seen no signs of life—none whatsoever—for blocks around.

He tried the door, and it opened. He stepped inside and looked around. Nothing but a big empty room with a couple of small offices partitioned off in one corner.

This didn't look like a fancy New York PR firm. That is to say, the investigator didn't know what the offices of a big, fancy New York PR firm would look like, but this couldn't be it.

And yet…he noticed the lights were on. They had already been on when he came in. Did that mean someone was there? Maybe the PR firm had a small satellite office in the building somewhere, or some storage space or something.

He walked in. Nothing at all was going on. But at one end of the building he found a door, which led to steps going down. And it was lit down there, too.

So the investigator, a little scared, cautiously went downstairs, stepping as carefully as he could so as not to make any noise. Halfway down, he heard a woman suddenly shriek in terror. The sound cut through his whole being, stopping his heart and paralyzing him for a horrible moment. He gathered his wits enough to turn around and try to stumble back up the stairs.

The female voice shouted, "HELP!"

The investigator stopped. If someone needed help, he should go back down and try to help her. But he had no idea what was going on. After all, this was New York City. Strange and exotic (not to mention grisly and unthinkable) crimes happened every day. He might be in over his head with this. He was frozen with indecision.

"HELP!"

Okay, he had to go down. He turned again and charged all the way down. The basement was as big as the upstairs, just a big open area with a concrete floor but without any windows. All the lighting came from a few sparsely placed fluorescent lights. In the distance, he could see a woman sitting at a desk, bolt upright, eyes unnaturally wide open, screaming. "HELP!"

He could also see that no one was attacking her. And then it hit him: she was scared of him. He stood still and slowly raised his hands to show that he was no threat.

"No, no," he pleaded. "I'm harmless, I promise."

"I'm sorry," the temp said, from way back in the back of the basement, her voice echoing and reverberating around. "It's just that I wasn't expecting anyone. Nobody ever comes in here."

He asked her about the PR firm he was looking for.

"Yes, this is the place," she said. "But I'm the only one here. All I do is check for e-mail and answer the phone. I've been here a month and I've only answered one call."

"Yesterday?"

"Yes. How did you know?"

"I was the one who called."

"Oh. So you have an appointment? I'm sorry, but you came to the wrong place."

"No, no appointment. I wanted to drop in by surprise."

"Well, you succeeded better than you could have

hoped for," the temp said.

"I called directory assistance to find out what address your phone number was located at. This is the address they gave me. They didn't have anything else listed for the firm."

"I'm sorry, but there's no one here but me."

He could see that. He could also see that something funny was going on. He already suspected that, though. What he could see here was that things were getting even funnier.

"This junior partner you connected me to on the phone. Where's he located?"

"I don't know. All I know is that they have an office somewhere, where everyone else works, but I don't know where it is. I don't even know why they want me here doing what I'm doing."

Yes, the investigator thought. This was fishy indeed. Highly suspicious.

"What number do you call when you have to call someone at the main office?"

"I don't think I'm allowed to give it out."

"Why not? A public relations firm would want their phone number to be available to the public, wouldn't they?" My goodness, the investigator thought. I'm "on" today.

"Well, I guess so." She wrote down the number and handed it to him.

And so another call to directory assistance got him the address for the non-fake fancy New York PR firm. He walked outside to the cab.

The address turned out to be a ritzy office suite located in a big, huge skyscraper. A fancy New York PR firm was located there, but it had a different name from the firm he had found in the warehouse.

The plot was deepening. The investigator felt as if he were in a movie. He pictured himself in close-up as he approached the door. Tight shot of his hand turning the doorknob. Cut to the reception area; the camera pans across the room to show a lot of chrome and black and glass in the decor, with modern art on the walls, pictures of lilies and pansies in a sort of semi-Oriental style; medium-long shot as he walks up to the receptionist's desk. Low angle as he asks the receptionist whether the junior partner he talked to yesterday is in.

Gosh, this movie stuff was fun. He'd have to do more of it when he got back home. Maybe it would be even more fun to do it when he played bouncy-bouncy with his wife.

"I think he just got back from a meeting," the receptionist said. "Just a moment and I'll check." She buzzed a button on her big control board and spoke into her headset. "Sir, there's a Mr.…" and then, to the investigator, "I'm sorry, I didn't get your name."

On a sudden flash of inspiration, the investigator told her he was the chairman of the mayor's political party.

"He says come on into his office," the receptionist said. "Down the hallway, third door on the left."

"Thank you."

The investigator walked past her desk, found the office, and knocked.

"Come in, come in, my friend," a friendly voice called.

The investigator opened the door and stepped in. The junior partner had already come halfway around his desk, hand extended, on his way to meet the visitor.

Then he stopped. "You're not..."

"No, I'm not. I'm not the chairman of the mayor's political party. I'm a private investigator working for the *opposing* party."

The junior partner's smile fell like a bag of wet sand into a freshly poured concrete floor.

CHAPTER SIX

On the mountainside, in his meditative state, the hermit approached the large building from across the parking lot. It appeared to be some sort of warehouse or something. He wasn't sure. He hadn't seen large buildings for, like, fifty years, so he couldn't be certain. He had thought that by now, in the real world at least, buildings would be sphere-shaped and fitted out with anti-gravity devices so they could float around in the air. Or not.

Above the door was a sign: 137. And on the door, THE SEVEN MISCHIEVOUS ELVES. That must be the name of this step, the hermit thought.

He stepped inside. It was a dim, forbidding place, full of dust and cobwebs. The hermit imagined that not even rats would want to come inside a place like this, just because it was so dreary. It was surprising that dark clouds weren't hovering over the building.

He walked around, kicking up dust, gazing at the huge windows that reached up almost to the high ceiling. In one corner, a couple of small offices had been partitioned off. At one end of the room, a door stood ajar.

He nudged the door open and saw stairs leading

down. Okay, this is it. Here goes. He walked down and found himself in a full basement, as large as the upper part of the building. It had a concrete floor and was badly lit.

And in the middle of the room were several people playing pin the tail on the goldfish. He didn't know it because he had never seen any of them in real life, but they looked like the mayor's daughter, her best friend, the mayor, the tall, manly guy, and the chairmen of both political parties.

The girl with wavy hair was the first to notice him. She stepped away from the group, who continued the game without any acknowledgement that he was there. "Would you care to join us?" she asked.

***

At the tall, manly guy's house, the tall, manly guy was watching TV with the mayor's daughter. The news people were reporting the new scandal.

"We received a tip that a big, fancy New York PR firm working for the mayor's political party actually manufactured a story we previously reported, about the opposing party launching a campaign to spread nasty rumors about the mayor's daughter."

"See?" the mayor's daughter said. "I'm really a good girl."

"Yes, you are," the tall, manly guy said.

"In fact," the reporter continued, "our sources tell us that the mayor's daughter's new boyfriend—that tall, manly guy—is actually an actor hired by the mayor's political party. He underwent extensive training and did lots and lots of studying and took special hormone shots just so he could make her fall in love with him..."

The anchor continued the story, but the mayor's daughter had heard as much as she needed to. "Is that true?" she asked. Well, it sounded more like a statement than a question, but grammatically it was a question.

This was, like, *totally* unexpected, and the tall, manly guy wasn't sure what to tell her. Everything had been cooking along so well, so utterly well, and now, all of a sudden, there was this. Somebody on TV was tipping her off that the whole thing was a fraud—unless he could talk her out of it.

"No, of course it's not true," the tall, manly guy said. "How could you even believe such a thing?" If he had been prepared for this, he could have reacted in a convincing way. As it was, he sounded sort of as if he were in a panic. A minor panic, to be sure, but a panic nonetheless.

"It's on TV, that's how."

"Well, the first story was on TV, the one that said you were wholesome, and now they're saying that one wasn't true. Someone has to be lying somewhere."

"What? You're saying I'm not wholesome?"

"Well, some people think..."

"Oh, I just don't know what to think," the mayor's daughter cried. "I just don't know."

The tall, manly guy leaned close and gave her a little kiss on the cheek. "Everything has been so great," he said. "Don't you trust me?"

And that decided it. His asking that question, in that way, could mean only one thing: he couldn't be trusted. "I think I have to go home now," she said. "I think it's time for us to break up."

Oh, no, the tall, manly guy thought. I can't let this happen. If she breaks up with me, I'm out of a job. But what could he say? He just totally wasn't prepared for this. His brain went into vapor lock.

The mayor's daughter stood up and went to the door. "I had a really nice time," she said. "Even if you're no longer my fella, if you decide to stay in the village, we can play bouncy-bouncy some more. I still think you're hot and stuff."

"Bouncy-bouncy?"

***

But of course, the tall, manly guy couldn't stay in the village after that. He was no longer of any use to the party, so he lost his cool job that didn't require him to do anything. He lost his cool house they had given him. If he was going to have to actually go back to work at a real job, he was, by golly, going to go back to New York City.

And that's what he did, but the mayor's daughter had ruined him. He was in love with her for the rest of his life—in love from afar.

***

At the Seven Mischievous Elves, all the pin the tail on the goldfish players were holding hands and dancing around the hermit, taunting him.

"You're ugly."

"Your mother dresses you funny."

"Where'd you get those *shoes*?"

The hermit had no idea what was going on. He

suspected something had gone wrong. He just couldn't figure out what.

"You smell funny, too. You smell like month-old French onion soup."

All these people were casting long shadows, directly away from the hermit, as if the light source were right above his head.

***

The chairman of the mayor's political party was blowing his top. Now, you might think it would hurt to blow his top, and in a way you'd be kinda right. The stuff that was going on in his head would ordinarily be painful, very painful, but he was so angry that he wasn't thinking about pain. He was thinking about the PR campaign blowing up in their faces.

He was ranting and raving. He was drooling all over his desk. He was seeing spots in front of his eyes. For a moment he even thought he saw a unicorn dancing with chipmunk, but that probably didn't have anything to do with being upset.

The chairman called his secretary at home. "This is an emergency," he shouted. "We have to have a meeting right away! Call all the party officials and tell them to meet me at party headquarters."

A half hour later, all the party officials, except for the mayor (who was, you'll remember, carefully kept out of the loop on matters such as this), were sitting around the conference table in the conference room at party headquarters. Most of them had seen the story on the news. The chairman gave a quick rundown of what had happened, as much as he knew, for the benefit of those who hadn't seen the story.

"We have to get out in front of this," the chairman said. "Any ideas?"

"Uh, what does it mean to get out in front of it?" someone asked.

"Why don't you just sit there and learn. Ideas, anyone else?"

"I think it's a pretty sure thing she'll dump this boyfriend, if she hasn't already," someone else said. "That means we'll have to find some other way to get her under control."

"Oh, gosh, it just doesn't let up, does it?" the chairman said. He sagged down into his chair.

***

Yes, and what about the village? This new scandal spread quickly, no big trick considering the story had been on TV. People went at this little juicy piece of info the way guys at a frat party go for the beer. Once again, people were abuzz. They were atwitter. They yip-yapped about it (yip-yapped?). Yes, the whole thing with the evil, nefarious plan to discredit the mayor, that whole thing was a made-up story designed to discredit the opposing party! Or something.

Yes, "or something." Because, you see, all this big fat mess was getting to be too much for most of them to follow.

People didn't know what to believe anymore. So although it was a good story, a story they liked to talk about, what they ended up believing was whatever the heck they wanted to believe. And for most of them, what they wanted to believe was whatever made the party they were registered with look good.

In other words, the stories about the opposing party and the mayor's party canceled each other out. It was a wash.

***

The village's reaction came as a big relief to officials of both parties because all of them, the officials, had been afraid that things would end up much worse, like with television crews from all over the world descending upon the village like Christmas shoppers at the local shopping mall on Black Friday, which would have been a great embarrassment to the entire village, and there would be a general outcry among the citizenry, maybe with riots and protests and demonstrations, and it was even possible that guys would end up in jail. That was what they had been afraid of.

Well, okay, so these little episodes caused the people of the village to become more cynical about their community leaders, but so what? If this stuff hadn't happened, something else would have. At least the party officials, all the way around, got through it without any disastrous results.

But one problem remained. And that problem was that the mayor's daughter had given the tall, manly guy the ol' heave-ho. He was out in the cold, and she was on the loose, on the prowl again. The mayor's party officials were going to have to do something about that.

So it was meeting time again. Ah, meetings, meetings.

Meetings.

***

At the soup kitchen, the mayor's daughter was talking to her best friend. "I can't believe it was all just a set-up," she said.

"It's a shame," the best friend said. "He seemed like such a great guy."

"It was nothing but an act. He acted as if he cared about me, but he didn't. It was just a job to him."

The best friend gave the mayor's daughter a quick little hug. "There, there," the friend said.

"I was even thinking we might get married. I thought daddy would be thrilled. He wanted me to stop…all the stuff I was doing."

"Can I have some mashed potatoes?" an old man asked. He held out his plate. The mayor's daughter dumped a blop of mashed potatoes on the plate, and he moved on.

"And all the time, he…daddy…was behind the whole thing. Can you *imagine* a more awful way to treat your own daughter, your own flesh and blood?"

"There is no more awful way," an unfamiliar voice said. The mayor's daughter and her best friend looked around. A sympathetic homeless lady was standing there. "Simply inexcusable," the lady said. The mayor's daughter gave her an extra-big blop.

The friend tried to assume the wisest, most serious look she could muster up. "You know," she said, "this doesn't mean you should go back to your misbehavioristic ways."

"Oh, how little you know," the mayor's daughter said.

***

"It's time we get serious," the chairman of the mayor's party said after he called the meeting to order. "We've been putzing and futzing around, doing all this nonsense kind of stuff, and as of tonight, we're pretty much back where we started."

"Except that the people of the village are now more cynical about their leaders," someone said.

"Yes, but we don't care about that as long as they're equally cynical about both parties. What we care about is the mayor's daughter's behavior."

And just as he said that, at that very moment, a gust of 90-mph wind hit the building, accompanied by a choir of voices (all of which sounded like Claude Rains) singing Joyce Kilmer's poem "Trees" to the tune of "Rhapsody in Blue." The temperature in the room rose by about twelve degrees. The paint started peeling from the walls—not a lot of it, just a little.

The party officials sat still, riding it out. When it was over—they weren't sure whether it had lasted just a few minutes or if it had gone on for hours because it was so confusing—they gathered their wits, set the table upright again, and (badly shaken) resumed the meeting.

"You know what that means," the chairman said.

"We need to get our rear ends in gear," someone said.

"Okay, suggestions?"

"Let's take up a collection to send her to college in New York City."

"Let's take up a collection to send her to college in San Francisco."

"Let's find some of that exotic paralyzing poison that comes from those plants in the jungle, and put some in her chewing gum."

"Won't work. She doesn't chew gum."

"How about a magic spell? I can make a couple of phone calls and find a witch doctor..."

"Too expensive."

"You know," the chairman said, "it occurs to me that we're looking at this problem backwards." He paused for effect. Everyone was looking at him expectantly. He had them hooked. "We've been trying to figure out how to control the girl. That's a mistake. We can't control her. That's like trying to control a frightened cat. No, what we need to do is control those guys."

"Ah, the guys," everyone whispered breathlessly, in unison.

"Yes, the guys. We need to control the guys. We need to make it so they don't want to play bouncy-bouncy with her."

"Bouncy-bouncy?" someone said.

"The way I see it," the chairman said, "we have to make them scared of her."

The others leaned in close. They could tell this was going to be a good plan.

***

The officials organized themselves into search parties. Because of the scary phenomena, they knew that at that very moment, somewhere out in the village (or in the general vicinity), some poor sap would be wandering around, delirious, lost, in a shallow sort of love. Their goal was to find him—or to put it more accurately, to get to him before anyone else did.

They combed the streets, up one way and down another, north and south, east and west, up and down, even diagonal. They looked behind buildings, and they looked behind bushes. They looked under parked cars. They looked in vacant lots, and they looked up in trees. They found six lost dogs and a stolen backhoe that had been abandoned by the thieves after a joyride. They found a case of oatmeal cookies. They found three crates of rusty power tools. They found a case of fake plastic puddles of vomit (that is to say, the vomit was fake, not the plastic). They found the copy of *The Tao of Pooh* that I lost years ago. I didn't need it back, though, because I bought a new one.

After an hour and a half, the party treasurer found the poor sap behind the television station, of all places. He was in the condition they had expected, with the added bonus that he was drooling. Sweet.

The treasurer manhandled the poor sap into his, the treasurer's, car. He drove away and hit the road out of the village. Five miles out, he stopped and texted the other party officials.

After everyone showed up—the five-mile place was their designated meeting spot—the party officials began the big intimidation process.

They got the poor sap down on the ground, face down, and held him there. That part was easy because of his weakened state. Then they beat him with the fake plastic puddles of vomit. You can't inflict much of a beating with fake vomit, but they didn't need much of a beating.

Then the verbal intimidation. "Listen, joker, if you even think about touching the mayor's daughter again, you'll get another beating. But next time we'll use fake dog poop."

"And we'll know if you think about it."

"We can tell."

"Don't think we can't."

"Yeah, buddy. You leave her alone from now on."

"Or you'll be sorry."

"And tell your friends they'll get the same treatment if they play with her."

"And don't tell anyone what happened here or we'll come back and get you again."

"Huh?" the poor sap said.

"Okay, well, you can tell your friends, but don't tell anyone else."

They drove the poor sap back to the village and dumped him out in front of the hair salon. He wasn't sure whether he was supposed to tell anyone what had happened or not, but he was sure he didn't want whatever had just happened to him to happen again. And if he did the wrong thing, it could happen again.

Best to play it safe and not say anything.

CHAPTER SEVEN

The mayor's daughter snuck in through her bedroom window and sat on her bed, sulking. It was stinky, just stinky, that daddy had set this whole thing up with the tall, manly guy. (Not having any reason to think that the party officials were really the ones who had fixed it all up, that was what she believed—that the mayor was behind the plan.)

Daggone him, anyway.

***

Meanwhile, at the Seven Mischievous Elves, the hermit was still in the middle of the ring of people making fun of him.

This is wrong, he thought. He concentrated hard, with all the considerable mental powers of his powerful mind, and he tried to come out of his meditative state.

It was more difficult than it should have been.

"Your nose is too big," someone was saying.

"Oh, and that hairstyle. It's, like, sooo ten years ago." And that was a hoot because ten years ago was still forty years ahead of any idea he might have had about hairstyles. For all he knew, people these days might be wearing their hair sculpted to look like rusty power tools. He didn't care, anyway.

What he cared about was coming out of his meditative state. He squenched his eyes shut as tight as possible. He made fists and dug his fingernails into his palms. He grunted.

The taunting took on an indistinct, far-away sound. The air began to feel fresher.

"Don't go away mad," a distant voice called.

"Just go away," another voice answered, followed by raucous laughter.

The hermit was fully awake now, sitting in his shack. He was dazed and breathless, not at all the way he usually felt after meditating. The room looked out of focus.

He blinked a few times and rubbed his eyes. His vision cleared up. He felt as if he had just awakened from a nightmare. He thought back to nightmares he had had as kid, one recurring nightmare in particular in which a large orange dragon had chased him through an amusement park, and the dragon carried a barrel of bacon grease under one arm, and with the other hand (claw) he scooped out great glops of grease and flung them at the then-hermit-to-be, lots of glops, rapid fire. And he would wake up tired, out of breath, and feeling greasy. He felt like that now, except without the grease.

The instructors at hermit school had never told him exactly what the meditative states would be like. In fact, they had said the experiences would vary greatly, so he had no way to say that what had happened was wrong. Nonetheless, he was sure that it was indeed wrong, wrong, wrong. He wasn't supposed to interact with people any longer than it would take to ask a question and get an answer. That was how it had always been—quick and businesslike.

Still, they had taught him to heed his instincts. This just felt wrong. And the bad thing, the really bad thing, was that he had no clue how to fix it. He didn't even know whether he *could* fix it. All he could do, as far as he could tell, was to desperately hope it would be better when he went back.

The hermit decided to go for a walk through the forest. Somehow, all the colors of the trees and the flowers were just a little less vibrant than usual. The sun seemed just a bit dim—just a bit; probably no one else would notice. The air, although much fresher than it had been at the Seven Mischievous Elves, still seemed a bit musty. The birds sounded as if they were singing in a minor key. He was sure he was back in the real world, yet it sort of seemed as if maybe the meditative state was somehow lingering on.

He came to an open pasture. He could look out over the top of the tall grass and see the village. Even if he was oh-so-slightly annoyed that it was there, he had to admit that it looked like a nice place to live for those who were inclined to live among other people.

***

And down in the village, the poor sap was in the hospital recovering. Angry and terribly upset, the mayor's daughter had been particularly rough on this guy. She had no desire to hurt him, but that didn't make it any easier. And as if that weren't enough, there was the fake vomit beating.

Yes, he was in much worse condition than other guys had been, and the hospital staff speculated as to why this might be. There had to be more to it than the run-of-the-mill finding of a delirious guy who had just gotten out of the clutches of the mayor's daughter. The consensus (at the hospital) was that it had something to do with the news stories about the political scandals, all of which had to do, directly or indirectly, with the mayor's daughter's behavior.

Anyway, the poor sap lay there in the hospital, watching TV with IVs stuck in him. Nurses took his pulse and gave him pills several times a day.

And he didn't say a word about what had happened, either with the mayor's daughter or with the party officials. All he had to do was recover and go about his life.

And pretend that nothing unusual had ever happened.

***

The chairman of the mayor's party talked to a couple of his most trusted and loyal police officers. He told them about what they had done to the poor sap. "What I need you to do," he said, "is be on the alert for any signs of mayor's daughter activity. When something happens, I need you guys to hit the streets and find the guy as soon as possible. Take him someplace and work him over. Intimidate him. Scare the poop out of him. Make sure he understands, in no uncertain terms, that it's in his best interests to leave the mayor's daughter alone from now on."

"Poop?"

"Out?"

"It's just a figure of speech. All I'm saying is make sure he's in a high state of being scared of her. If he sees her out in public, I want him to run home, lock his door, and spend the rest of the day trembling like a Dutch vibrator, looking nervously up to the ceiling expecting an iron fist to come crashing through, out of the heavens, and mash him into the floor. Any questions?"

"What's a Dutch vibrator?"

"Actually, I don't think there's any such thing. It just sounded good."

"Don't they make vibrators in the Netherlands?"

"I'm sure they do. But I doubt that there's anything special about them."

"Well, you know, it depends on how you use them. I was reading on this one web site..."

"I don't care," the chairman snapped. "It doesn't matter. All I'm saying is, if there are more signs of activity, find the guy and scare him real good, okay?"

"Okay."

As soon as the police officers were gone, the chairman went to his computer and searched for "special way to use a vibrator" on the Internet.

***

The hermit was afraid to go back into meditation. He had no idea what would happen. Maybe those strange people were waiting for him with knives and chain saws, ready to attack. Maybe they'd throw bacon grease at him. He could think of all sorts of unpleasant things they might do. They might beat him with plastic puddles of vomit.

Huh? How did he think of *that*?

And so he sat around knocking back the carrot wine as if he were deathly afraid the police were about to stage a raid and throw him in the dungeon for life if they found any traces of alcohol in his shack.

Between drinks, he sang old songs from his younger days. Well, that is to say, he sang small portions of songs because he didn't leave much time between drinks. He sang portions of songs like "Let's Go Drive Some Backhoes Around" and "Two, Four, Six, Eight, How Many Cookies Have You Ate?" (The songwriter explained in numerous interviews for years afterward that he tried for weeks to find a grammatically correct way to get the word "ate" at the end of the sentence, and he finally just gave up.)

The drinking and singing distracted him. He knew, however, that he would eventually have to go back to the Seven Mischievous Elves.

***

The mayor's daughter had been avoiding her daddy. She was just so mad that she didn't know what she would say to him. She could think of a few things she would like to say, but she knew better than to say them.

It couldn't go on forever, though. She came home from work one day, and he was sitting there waiting for her. "Why have you been avoiding me?" he asked.

"Because of that awful thing you did," she said, and breezed by him and went upstairs.

The mayor sat on the sofa for a moment digesting what had just happened. Awful thing he had done? What could that have been? He knew that as a politician he had undoubtedly done a whole lot of things that people would consider awful, but he didn't know what things she knew about that he had done, or what she would consider awful.

Had it been that inside deal with the kickbacks to build badger houses in the public park? Or the inside deal with kickbacks to build floodwalls across the top of the nearby mountain? No, no, neither of those. It had to be the inside deal with the kickbacks to hire an artist to make an eighty-foot sculpture of a tumbleweed next to the main highway where it entered the village. Yeah, that was it.

Or maybe she had found out about his counterfeit shoelace operation. He'd been running it for more than seven years now, since before he'd become mayor, hiring people at less than minimum wage to make knockoffs of all the top-brand designer shoelaces. With it going on that long, it was possible—likely, even—that she would have found out about it.

And then there was the normal stuff like nepotism, no-bid government contracts, bribery for mundane things like zoning changes and such. Maybe she'd found out he was selling off surplus office supplies online and pocketing the money.

Well, really, he could think of dozens of possibilities. Best thing was to talk to her. Going upstairs, he had a bad moment when he was afraid that she had discovered he was collecting protection money from that black market diuretic paint thinner ring. He really, really wouldn't want her to know that he was involved in anything like diuretic paint thinner, highly dangerous substance that it was, even in an indirect way such as allowing the dealers to operate.

He knocked on her door, and it occurred to him that

she might have found out that he was letting a large manufacturing company truck toxic waste in and bury it at the town dump. A minor earth tremor could very well cause the drums to break open and spill hazardous chemicals into the ground, rendering the village and the surrounding area uninhabitable for the next thirty thousand years. But they were paying him checks with lots of zeroes on them, yes sir.

When his daughter answered her door, she seemed surprised to see that it was him. "Oh, it's you. What do you want?" she asked.

"I want to know why you're mad at me."

"Because you're a scummy piece of hamster poop," she said.

"I'm sorry. That doesn't give me any information I can work with. What did I do?" Maybe she had learned about *everything*. Even the deal with the arms smugglers who were posing as traveling performance artists.

"Okay, if you want me to say it, I will. You hired that tall, manly guy and trained him to make me fall in love with him. How could you do such an awful thing?"

Holy smoke, he thought. With all the things he had done that she could rightfully be upset about, she was angry over something he *hadn't* done? "Listen, sweetie, I don't know what you're talking about."

The mayor's daughter's face got all red. She hyperventilated. Her hair grew a sixteenth of an inch. The hair growth didn't have anything to do with being mad, but it happened anyway.

She slammed the door in his face.

"Does this mean you don't want to talk about it?" he asked.

***

Even madder now, the mayor's daughter got dressed to impress, did her makeup, brushed her hair, and took off to go to the tavern. By golly, if he didn't want her messing around with guys, that was *exactly* what she was going to do.

Ha!

She tromped downstairs, blew right by her daddy, and went out the door before he could say anything. (Now, the attentive reader might be wondering how she had previously snuck in and out through her window if her room is on the second floor. I don't have a good answer for that. I know it's lame, but let's just say she had a rope ladder. If you have a better idea, just go ahead and assume that your better idea is what she did.)

She went down to the tavern and staked out her place at the bar. She was mad, angry, and irate, and everyone there could tell. It was coming off of her in waves, and they could feel it. If the lighting had been a bit better, they could have seen disturbances in the air around her as the waves emanated outward.

People felt awkward at first, but after a few minutes they recovered and were able to go about their drinking and talking and dart playing and such.

The mayor's daughter spotted a guy who looked good and approached him. "You. Me. Home," she said.

The guy shrugged. "Sure," he said.

At this point it might be good to mention, just so you don't have the wrong idea, that not all the guys in the village were mindless sex automatons who were just sitting there waiting for the mayor's daughter to come and pluck them off their barstools as if she were picking flowers. No, many of them had wives or girlfriends, and they were faithful to their women. Many felt that the casual playing of bouncy-bouncy was an empty and meaningless experience and preferred to get to know a young lady before indulging in such behavior. Some were gay. The thing is, we're just not concerned about those guys.

Anyway, back to the story. The mayor's daughter went home with the guy. As they went up to his room, his landlady saw that the mayor's daughter was with him. She ran to her kitchen and nervously packed away all her valuable china, well padded, to protect it. Unfortunately, her hands were shaking so badly that she broke two plates and a cup.

In the guy's room, he and the mayor's daughter unleashed the usual forces of nature. Earthquakes, tornadoes, yadda yadda. You know the routine. The landlady was afraid they had compromised the structural integrity of the building. She made a note to call someone first thing in the morning to come out and inspect it. Would the insurance company pay for damage caused by this kind of stuff?

While the landlady was worrying about her building, the guy was out somewhere in the village, now abandoned by the mayor's daughter, rolling around on the ground oh so slowly because he didn't have enough strength left to work up a respectable roll-around; in fact, even though he thought he was rolling around, a casual observer would have described it as a series of intermittent motions that resembled someone having a horrible nightmare in super slow motion.

The police friends of the party chairman, having been alerted by the usual signs, were out searching for the poor sap. They went through the village, conducting their search as thoroughly as possible. They found three stolen cars, a pin the tail on the goldfish game, some exercise equipment cleverly modified to resemble sculptures of jungle animals, a man who had been hiding from his wife for the last three and a half years (he hadn't meant for it to last that long; he just lost track of time)...

...and the poor sap. "Hey, look over there," one of the officers said. "I think that's him, jerking around in the grass."

"That's not jerking. It's too slow to be jerking."

"Spazzing out, maybe?"

"No. I'd say it's more like he's twisting around."

"Herb, would you call it twisting around?"

"No, that's not twisting."

"Definitely not twisting."

"Oh, what do you know?"

They took the poor sap to an abandoned warehouse on the outskirts of the village. The party chairman had set up a small hospital ward in the basement where they could take all the poor saps, and no one would know where they were. No one would go into the warehouse because it was all old and decrepit looking, and if they did, they surely wouldn't go down to the basement. And if someone happened to go down there anyway...well, you can take only so many precautions.

They put the guy in bed and rigged him up with an IV to replenish his fluids. That was one of the big problems these guys had, these poor saps: all of them suffered from dehydration. Strange, it was, that someone could get to such a state in such a short time, but there it was.

Unfortunately, the party didn't have any doctors as part of its inner circle. The secretary of the party claimed to "know a little something about medicine," so he was to be the one in charge of watching over the poor saps who were brought there. What the other officials didn't know was that "know a little something about medicine" meant that he had seen commercials on TV saying that if you're having a heart attack, it's a good idea to take some aspirin. But there's more to medicine than that. Fortunately, these poor saps didn't need much more medical care than bed rest and fluids. When the hospital kept them for a few days, it was only for observation; no one had suffered any complications because otherwise they were all strong, healthy fellas.

They, the party officials, also strapped the poor sap down because they wanted to make sure he couldn't run away as soon as he got strong enough. They had plans for this guy.

***

While this strapping was going on, the mayor's daughter, still blindingly angry at her father, returned to the tavern. She was coming back for seconds. Her normal rate was once or twice a week, so twice in one night was unheard of. Simply unheard of. (And fortunately for the first guy's landlady, this second guy lived in a different building.)

So it was that in the warehouse, as the party officials were putting the finishing touches on strapping down the poor sap, a subsonic vibration cut through the air, accompanied by a sound that was like a chorus of cats wailing in mourning, except that the wailing sounded something like a very rough rendition of the Grateful Dead's "New Speedway Boogie." Unknown to the people in the warehouse basement, all the birds flew out of the village. (They would come back the next day.)

"Oh, gosh, we're going to have another one coming in," the chairman said.

And after thinking they were home for the night, all settled down in front of the TV with beer and deep-fried chicken fat snacks, the police officers wearily dragged themselves out for another search. This time they were tired and cranky, and they wanted nothing more than to be back home relaxing, so they didn't find anything extra. Well, except for those two mail bags full of baby carrots. But that was all. Oh, and Ambrose Bierce. They found him, and that was noteworthy.

So on the first night of this new crusade: two poor saps in the improvised ward, delirious, not sure where they were, strapped down and hooked up to IVs. And the secretary gave them aspirin, just to make sure.

***

Home, the mayor's daughter considered going back for thirds, but it was almost time for her favorite TV show, *Herman the Gyrating Tortoise.* She knew, though, she knew that her daddy had heard/felt/seen two sets of... uh, experiences. He surely knew the score. She had made her point.

***

At the hospital, the emergency room staff was ready for two new patients. They were waiting. They were just standing around waiting.

***

The chairman of the mayor's party, at home, was frothing at the mouth. He was prowling around the house like a hungry tiger, frantic, desperate. Two in one night! That was beyond the pale!

He wanted to call another meeting, he desperately wanted to. He had the strongest urge to call people and get them to go to headquarters, to the conference room, and maybe even include the mayor this time, that useless goofball. What the chairman wanted to do was to do *something*. He felt the need to be proactive. Even though he had a plan underway, he was having trouble finding the patience to see it through because at this point all he could do was sit tight and let it play out.

His wife was terribly concerned. She wanted him to sit down. She offered him a little special beverage to help him relax. She asked him whether he wanted to play bouncy-bouncy. None of it was any good.

Like many people—like far too many people—he was simply wound too daggone tight.

***

On his mountainside, the hermit was out for another walk. It had been two days since that frightful experience at the Seven Mischievous Elves—and if that was mischievous, he hated to think what malevolent would be like!

As he walked, he thought about his problem. He knew he had to go back and resume his journey, but it was unpleasant just to think about it. For the first time, the first time in fifty years, he actually dreaded meditation.

He stopped walking for a moment and watched a butterfly flit about. Yeah, that butterfly had no problems. It just did what it did.

The hermit thought about the training he'd received at hermit school. He thought about the classes he'd taken and tried to recall something that might apply to this. He'd taken meditation classes (Meditation I, II, and III, covering all aspects of theory and technique), problem-solving, logic, structure of the spiritual world, mapping of the spiritual world, physics of the spiritual world, denizens of the spiritual world...yes, maybe he'd learned something there? But no. The instructor had been very clear on one point. They would never interact with the denizens of the spiritual world beyond a very brief, businesslike exchange of a question and answer. The instructor had not simply said the interaction *shouldn't* be more than that, he had said it *couldn't* be more.

He looked through his textbooks: *The History and Lore of the Hermit Way*; *Meditations and Musings on Life as a Hermit*; *Mulligan and McSnoot's Guide to the Spiritual World* (Vols. 1 through 4); *The Lives of Seven Famous Hermits*; *Overcoming Everything You've Ever Known and Leaving It Behind*, and so on. It was interesting to look through books he hadn't opened in many years, but he found nothing of help.

He considered writing a letter to the advice column

in *Modern Hermit* magazine to ask what he should do. The problem was that he couldn't wait for the letter to go through the editorial process, and maybe not get chosen for publication, but if it was, he might not see the answer for two or three months, or however long it would take. He needed an answer *now*.

The hermit was on his own, with a problem that nothing had ever prepared him for.

***

In the basement of the warehouse—the hospital ward warehouse, not the meditative state warehouse that had the hermit all discombobulated or the warehouse where the fake fancy New York PR firm was located—the two poor saps had recovered from their adventures with the mayor's daughter.

One night the party secretary gave them a sedative, to make sure they would sleep very deeply indeed, that they would sleep the sleep of the innocent (although, as we have seen, they were far from innocent), so a special group of flunkies working for the party could do what they were going to do without any concern over waking the poor saps up.

And what the flunkies did was hoist the beds up, flip them around upside down, and bolt the beds to the ceiling.

When the poor saps woke up, they were all alone and scared. They screamed. They shouted. They were sure they were going to fall, but the beds were very securely bolted, and the poor saps were very securely strapped to the beds.

The party officials left them like that for a couple

more hours, just to scare them, just to drive the point home.

Finally, two of the police officers who were friendly with the party chairman came to visit them.

"Hi, how's it going?" the first officer said.

"Do you mean, 'How's it going after the mayor's daughter put me through the most exhausting experience of my life and left me for dead, and now I'm strapped to a hospital bed that's bolted upside down to the ceiling in some dingy basement somewhere with a concrete floor for some reason I can't imagine?' Is that what you mean?"

"Yeah, sure. We can go with that," the police officer said.

"Pretty rotten."

"Aw, I'm sorry to hear that. What's wrong?"

The poor sap sighed and shook his head.

"Okay," the other officer said, "I can see you're in no mood to play games. You want to cut right to the chase. Is that it?"

"Yeah, I'd say that's it."

"A man of action. That's what I like."

"That's what I like, too," the other officer said. "A man of action."

"But don't get any ideas, buddy," the first officer said. "We don't like you *that* way."

"I wasn't getting any ideas."

"Okay, so we understand each other."

"I don't understand anything," the second poor sap said, speaking for the first time. "I just want down from here."

"How did you like your date with the mayor's daughter?" the first officer asked.

"Huh?" the two poor saps said in unison. They were almost, but not quite, in harmony. With just a little practice, maybe they could harmonize very well.

"The mayor's daughter. Did you have a good time with her?"

"I think I'm in love," the first poor sap said.

"Hey, you rotten stinker," the second poor sap said. "*I'm* in love with her."

"Yeah? Well, you just wait till we get out of here, buddy. I'll pound you so bad she won't know who you are."

"Oh, listen to Mister Solve-Everything-By-Fighting. She likes me better because I'm more refined and sophisticated."

"She doesn't care about that. She likes a man of action."

"Shut up, you two," the first police officer said. "Just shut the heck up. She doesn't like either one of you. You don't mean any more to her than the bowl she ate her cereal out of this morning."

"She showed me her cereal bowl," the first poor sap said. "It's a Bert the Badger bowl, and it's her favorite. She loves that bowl." He was making up the story, of course. Remember, they had gone to *his* place; she couldn't have shown him her Bert the Badger bowl.

"Oh, yeah?" the other poor sap said. "Well, I'm the one who gave it to her!"

"I said shut up!" the first police officer shouted. Everyone fell silent, the way a rowdy class of schoolchildren who had been left unattended will suddenly stop misbehaving when the teacher comes back, but the big difference here was that very few teachers rig up their kids so they're hanging from the ceiling. Sometimes the kids do that to one another, but that's a different story.

At any rate, a feeling of awkwardness washed over the basement, the same sort of "oh, we went too far" awkwardness that washes over a classroom when the aforementioned teacher comes back. The two poor saps expected to get sent to the chalkboard to write a sentence a hundred times.

The first police officer glared at the poor saps. Seeing that they were (apparently) going to behave themselves now, he nodded in satisfaction. "Okay," he said. "Here's how it is. It must be obvious to you that we can do anything we want to you."

"You'd better not," the second poor sap said in his best "Oh yeah? Yo mama," tone of voice.

"I suggest you think about that some more," the second officer said.

The first poor sap did some thinking, and let me tell you what he thought. He thought that the police officers could do anything they wanted to them. He also thought that his best chance at getting out of there was to be agreeable. "Yes," he said. "I can see that you can do anything you want to us."

"Good," the first police officer said. "No one knows where you are—"

"You do," the second poor sap said.

"No one knows where you are," the officer reiterated. "No one would ever know what happened to you if you were never to come out of this basement."

"What do you want?" the first poor sap said.

"What do I want," the officer echoed. "That's what I like to hear. Willingness to cooperate." He paused for effect, puffing his chest out so as to look more important.

"What I want—what certain powerful people in this village want—is for the mayor's daughter to behave herself. You guys know you're not the only ones she's played with. You know she's quite the social butterfly, right?"

"Uh, yeah, I've heard stories."

"I'm sure you have. Everyone has. So here's the deal. She's not going to behave herself. She's going to do what she wants to do, and we can't stop her. So we're going about solving the problem from the other direction. We want to cut off her supply, so to speak."

"Her supply?"

"Her supply of young fellas to play bouncy-bouncy with. If no one's willing to play with her, she has no choice but to behave herself, does she?"

"Uh...is this a trick question?"

"No, not at all. It's a question that means you need to leave her alone. If she asks you to play with her again, you need to tell her you can't. Tell her you won't. If you have to, tell her your weewee fell off."

"My weewee?"

"It doesn't matter what you tell her. The important thing is that you'd better not touch her. If you do, you'll end up back here again. And you won't come back out."

"Okay," said the first poor sap.

"Okay," said the second poor sap. He was beginning to understand the true nature of his situation.

"And if you happen to tell your friends what we told you, it might save them some grief. You're lucky that we're letting you off with a warning the first time. Pretty soon, if this keeps up, we're going to start making guys disappear the first time we catch them."

"That's not fair," the second poor sap said.

"Then you'd better let your friends know what's going on."

***

That night the hermit had a dream. He was working in a large warehouse, feverishly driving a forklift around, looking for cartons and crates and eventually finding them in the wrong areas after too many wrong turns through the aisles, but finding he was unable to pick them up with the forklift because they were sitting flat on the floor rather than stacked on pallets…

He finally gave up and turned off the forklift. He fought back tears of frustration. He got up and walked around the warehouse. From a distance he could hear laughing and shouting, as if a party were going on. Following the noise, he came to the employee break room. As he entered, the partiers—they were the pin the tail on the goldfish players from the Seven Mischievous Elves—fell silent. "Well, I guess it's time to get back to work," one of them said, eyeballing the hermit with a sort of low-level hostility.

They stood up and filed through the doorway, elbowing their way not too politely past the hermit. The cute girl with wavy hair was last. As she got to the door, she stopped. "I'll see you later," she said to him.

***

And in real life, apart from anything happening in the spiritual world or in the hermit's dreams—in the flesh-and-blood physical world, the mayor's daughter was having her own problems. Word was spreading among the young fellas about the threats the police officer had made. She was finding it difficult to recruit new guys for games of bouncy-bouncy, difficult indeed.

But a few guys hadn't heard about the threats. So after a couple hours of trolling through the tavern, she found a willing partner who was ready to take her home.

As they walked out together, other guys tried to warn him. "Hey, you'd better not take her home," they said, a lot of guys over and over again as he walked to the door with the mayor's daughter. "You'll disappear and never be seen again."

But he was wise to them, yes sir. They were jealous that he was about to score with this smokin' hot babe. They wanted to scare him off so they could take shot at her. But he wasn't going to fall for it. He wasn't stupid.

***

The next day he learned that he wasn't nearly as smart as he had thought. That is to say, he found out what you and I already knew: he shoulda listened to those warnings when he left the tavern.

He found himself strapped to a bed that was bolted upside down...well, you know the scene. When he regained consciousness, he knew immediately that he was in deep trouble. "This is bad," he thought. "That girl was wild, no doubt about it, but I don't think *this* was her idea." Then he started thinking, going off on a train of thought wondering what it would have been like if the mayor's daughter had wanted to fix him up this way. What would she have done then? How would she have used this particular...situation...as part of their fun and games? Thinking about it made him excited, something he didn't want under the circumstances.

Daggone it, he didn't even have anything to read.

They left him there, stuck to the ceiling, for a whole day, all alone in that basement. Then the flunkies came in to get him down. He tried to get them to tell him what was going on, but they said they didn't know anything. Hey, they were just there to do a job, okay?

When the police officers came in to talk to the poor sap, they acted very angry.

"We are sooo angry with you," the first one said.

"You are in sooo much trouble," the second one said.

"How dare—*how dare*—you play bouncy-bouncy with the mayor's daughter."

"It was her idea."

"And I suppose it was someone else's idea for you to say yes, eh?"

"Huh?"

"Well, buddy boy, you've overplayed your hand. You've overplayed it very gladly. I mean badly."

"I'd say gladly and badly," the second officer said.

"You're never leaving this room again," the first officer said.

"You can't do that," the poor sap said.

The first police officer sat down and lit a cigarette. He puffed casually. He wished he had a white cat sitting in his lap to pet. "Oh, but we can," he purred. Daggone, he just *knew* he looked cool.

"We can and we will," the other officer said.

Then they decided to work him over. They beat him with fake vomit. They threw ice water on him. They brought a bunch of dogs in to bark at him. By the end of the day, he was nothing more than a quivering mass of warm pudding. And he was convinced they were going to do the same thing every day for the rest of his miserable life.

But the next day they came back and said they were going to release him. "I think we made our point," the first police officer said.

"Oh, yes. Yes, indeed," the poor sap said. He went home to recover and then told his friends about his awful experience.

***

Word got around the village some more. When the mayor's daughter came back to the tavern a couple days later, everyone shied away from her. She sat at the bar, and no one would come close enough for her to talk to them. Not even the women. (It's not that they were scared of her; they were just scared of her in the tavern, the place where she was known to find her playmates.)

What was going on? She sat there with her drink, drinking, looking around. No one would even meet her glance. This was very strange.

After finishing her drink, the mayor's daughter decided to give up. She slowly made her way to the door. Behind her, she was sure she could hear a collective sigh of relief.

Had someone been spreading rumors about her?

Outside, she saw a guy coming toward the entrance. "Hey there," she said.

It just so happened that he was one of the few who hadn't heard about the dire threats. He smiled. "Hi, yourself," he said.

"What are you up to tonight?" she asked.

"Nothing much. You got any ideas?"

"I have plenty of ideas," the mayor's daughter said. "Plenty."

Of course, you know what happened. There was the usual array of natural and unnatural phenomena, along with some unnatural variations of what would otherwise have been natural phenomena. The police friends of the party chairman searched and found the poor sap and took him to their secret underground hideout, the warehouse basement, and did the upside-down-bed-on-the-ceiling thing, etc., etc., etc.

They didn't let this guy go.

***

"It was very strange," the mayor's daughter told her best friend at the soup kitchen. "No one would talk to me in the tavern. It's almost as if they were scared of me."

The best friend had gotten wind of the threats, or should we say the rumors of the threats. She didn't know how to tell the mayor's daughter about them, though. She didn't even know if she should tell her. Maybe she should just let it go, pretend she didn't know. It wouldn't make any difference, the best friend thought, in regard to how all this played out.

"Yes, that's very strange," the best friend said.

"Have you heard anything, any rumors or stories?" the mayor's daughter asked.

"No, I haven't."

"I have," an old man said, holding out his plate for

some creamed rutabagas.

"No, you haven't," the best friend said, giving him a glop.

"But..." he said.

The best friend shot him a threatening look, and he shuffled away.

"What was that all about?" the mayor's daughter asked.

"Oh, you know," the best friend said. "Rumors spread in places like this. I don't know what they've been saying, but I'm sure it couldn't be true. So I don't want you to worry about it."

"You're such a good friend."

"I'm just trying to look out for you."

They served a few more people.

"What am I going to do if I can't find any more playmates?" the mayor's daughter asked.

"Well, you might want to think about finding a nice guy and having a meaningful relationship."

The mayor's daughter thought about that one for a few moments. "Yeah, right," she said.

That made the best friend think it might be better to tell the mayor's daughter about the threats. Maybe it was best if she knew the reality of her situation. But the best friend would have to frame it just right. "Well, okay, I'll tell you something," she said. "I didn't want to say anything because I didn't know how much truth there is to it, but now I think you should probably know about it."

The mayor's daughter stopped serving. "What is it?"

"There are rumors—strictly unsubstantiated rumors," the best friend said, "that guys you've been playing with have been taken to a secret underground location and threatened and tortured. They say one guy disappeared completely, never seen again."

"So they *are* afraid of me," the mayor's daughter said. "Wow. Just, wow."

***

The mayor's daughter went back to the tavern that night and got the big freeze-out, just like last time, except that this time there was no one who was unaware of the danger and just happened to come along at the right time. She struck out.

Next night, same thing. She came back home, frustrated and angry. She confronted her father. "Have you been threatening the guys in the village?" she asked.

"What?"

"No one will talk to me at the tavern. They're scared of me. What have you been doing?"

"I haven't done anything."

She glared at him. He looked at her blankly. She sighed and relented. It seemed clear to her that he didn't have anything to do with it. And really, now that she thought about it, that type of devious plot didn't seem like his style. It was just a little too clever for him. But someone else might be behind it all. "It's the officials who run your political party, isn't it?" She knew those guys, the chairman and his cronies, were pretty devious.

"I don't know, sweetheart. I really don't know. Maybe."

PART TWO: THE HERMIT

CHAPTER EIGHT

The hermit had been born some seventy-odd years ago—an expression not meant to imply that the years themselves were odd, although many of them, in fact, were. Well, *most* of them were, if you must know.

As a small child, he was fairly ordinary in most respects. When he got big enough, he went to school and had friends and whatnot. It became apparent to his parents that he was maybe a bit brainier and more... uh, shall we say, more introspective than average, but to be brutally honest, no one else paid enough attention to him to notice. He was kind of a nondescript kid.

Throughout his childhood, he never thought about becoming a hermit. He didn't know anything about hermits. He thought about becoming, maybe, a hair stylist or a flute teacher. Or maybe the mayor of a small village. He thought it might be an interesting job, mayor of a small village. He could rule mercilessly, with an iron fist. He could issue commands and demands and decrees, and everyone would have to obey. He could order his flunkies around to carry out his every whim. Maybe the flunkies could be a select group of officers on the local police force. A small village would be about right, he thought—and this is surprisingly sophisticated thinking for a small child, I would say—because he could keep on top of everything that would happen and maintain control better. In a city, you have more excitement and more money and more beautiful women, but you also have more enemies and, in general, more things you simply can't account for.

So being the mayor of a small village seemed more to his liking. He read books about politics and what it was like to be a mayor, and he thought it all sounded really neat. But it nagged at him in the back of his mind that there might be a downside that he didn't know about.

He went on for a while with his mayor interest, unusual for a kid but not really all that weird. He joined the chess club. Hey, some people thought that was weirder than being interested in becoming a mayor someday.

It was sometime when he was about ten or eleven that he started hiding. He would hide in the closet, in the basement, in the tool shed in the backyard. He would let his parents look for him for a while, and when they were off somewhere else searching he would sneak back to his room, stretch out on the bed with a book about being a mayor, and pretend he had been there all along.

One day when he was staying with his grandmother, he sat down under the dining room table, with the tablecloth hanging down so he couldn't be seen by anyone who didn't think to get down on hands and knees to look underneath. And that, indeed, was exactly what his grandmother didn't think of doing. She searched frantically, scared that someone had snatched him out of the front yard or something. She looked all over the house. She walked up and down the street and then got in her car and drove around the block. She called the police. It was only then that he thought he'd better come out.

After that, the hiding sessions became longer and more frequent. He hid at school, and the teacher would think he had run away. School officials talked to his parents. His parents talked to him. He talked to...well, to no one. The school punished him. His parents punished him. But what did he care about punishment? Hiding was more important. As he continued hiding, he gradually lost interest in becoming a mayor. In most cases, you can't be an effective mayor if you're running off and hiding several times a day.

Everyone assumed he was doing all this hiding just to get people to search for him so he could be the center of attention and then enjoy the "Oh, there you are!" moment when they found him. Yes, attention, they thought.

He didn't think about it much, at least not at the time, but he knew that it wasn't for attention. That was the last thing he wanted. (It was only from their own self-centered point of view that the adults assumed he was doing all this hiding for the sake of attention. Adults have a way of thinking children do just about everything they do to get attention, but to be fair, with most children, most of the time, that's exactly what it's all about.)

It was later, as a teenager, that the hermit—or should we say hermit-to-be—came to understand that he was hiding simply for the sake of hiding. He wanted to get away from people. He wanted to be by himself. It wasn't good enough just to shut himself up in his room, lock the door, and read or whatever. He didn't want anyone to know where he was.

Truly, he had the makings of a great hermit.

He moved out of his parents' house as soon as he was able. His new place was a small room above a hair salon. It was nice because at night no one else was in the building. He worked as a flute teacher for a while. As time went on, the hermit-to-be realized that this was more human contact than he would like, but at least he had to deal with only one person at a time.

Don't get me wrong. The hermit-to-be had friends. He just didn't hang out with them very much. They just knew him as an "all right kinda guy" who was fairly quiet. He wasn't around much, but he was likeable.

All through this, through the little-room-living and the flute teaching, the hermit-to-be was looking for another job, one that wouldn't require him to deal with anyone else at all. He wanted a job that would allow him to do whatever he had to do completely by himself.

Think about it: that's a pretty tall order.

Now, he never told his friends about his desire to be alone. They hadn't discussed it among themselves. It just sort of happened one day that a friend showed him an ad, simply because he thought it would be funny, a good joke that everyone in their little circle of friends would get. It was a small ad in the back of a magazine, just a few lines:

Learn to be a hermit!
An unusual career for unusual people!
Nine-month course makes you an expert!
Easy financing available!

Under that was a phone number punctuated with an exclamation point. Normally, phone numbers aren't punctuated with anything at the end, so clearly this number was special.

Anyway, the bit with the ad was just intended as a joke. Everyone was supposed to chuckle and then forget about it. But for him, the hermit-to-be, it was a revelation. He thought that being a hermit would be his ideal job, the job he had wanted all along. He hadn't known that it could be a viable career path. Maybe it was, though. They had put the word "career" right there in the ad.

"Can I have that ad?" the hermit-to-be asked.

The friend was taken aback. "Huh?"

"Can I have that ad?"

"Uh, sure."

The hermit-to-be took the magazine home, and the next day he called the number.

They put him through a series of rigorous tests. They gave him written tests: multiple choice, true-false, essay questions, and so on. They gave him physical tests to determine his strength and endurance. They gave him psychological tests. They dunked him in water, telling him it was a test but really doing it just because they thought it was funny. They told him he was one of their highest-scoring pre-screening test-takers ever. It would be an unthinkable waste of talent if he didn't become a hermit.

He beamed in happiness over that. They were saying he showed a very high aptitude for a career that seemed to be made just for him.

He arranged for transcripts of his high school report cards to be sent to hermit school.

He had enough money saved up to make a down payment on his tuition and student fees, but that was all. They had him fill out a lot of financial aid forms to apply for grants and student loans and such. It was going to cost him everything he had to become a hermit, but so what? As a hermit he wasn't going to need much in the way of material goods, anyway. He was going to eschew worldly things.

He liked that word, eschew.

Eschew. Gesundheit.

Anyway, the hermit-to-be made all the arrangements and finally ended up enrolled as a full-time student at hermit school. He lived on campus, which he thought kind of odd. That is to say, they had all their students living together as they learned how to live alone.

But that was okay. It was even okay that the school put the students into study groups for some of the courses so they could help one another learn how to live alone.

Let it be said, here and now, that hermit school was a scam. Yes, I know. You've already figured that out. Hermit school? Come on, get serious.

Still, some of the students managed to get valuable knowledge from it. And our hermit-to-be was one of them. He buckled down and studied hard and worked his rear end off. He learned all the secrets of such legendary hermits as Chester Shy and Mortimer Stylite.

He did his reading, passed tests, did projects, made in-class presentations. He did the lighting for the school play, a rousing performance of *Our Town*.

He served a one-year apprenticeship under the guidance of one of the most famous hermits of all, Alvin

Loner. Alvin was known far and wide, in hermit circles, for his superhuman ability to devote himself to the hermit way of life with an exceedingly narrow, laserlike focus. He had contributed a number of articles to *Modern Hermit* magazine, but his level of achievement was so far above everyone else's that even though he tried to make his articles as simple as possible, no one could understand them.

There was even a persistent rumor that famous film director Werner Herzog had, at one time, been interested in making a movie that would chronicle Alvin's life and times. Herzog wanted to document Alvin's achievements and his triumphs over the trials and tribulations that led to the downfall of too many (far too many) hermits.

Alvin agreed "in principle" to the idea of making the movie. What did he care? But true to form, he refused to meet with Herzog. He wouldn't even agree to a five-minute meeting to sign a contract for the rights to his story.

Without the contract (according to the persistent but unsubstantiated story), investors backed out. They were afraid that Alvin would sue after the movie was released. Herzog explained to them that that was the last thing, the very last thing ever, that Alvin would consider doing. He wasn't interested in the money, and besides, suing would mean he'd have to show up in court, and there was no chance of that.

Still, the investors were skittish. They diverted the money for their Alvin Loner movie investment into a remake of *Ma and Pa Kettle in Waikiki*, and the Alvin Loner movie was forever after to be no more than a rumor.

Our hermit-to-be had read this story in *Modern Hermit*. He didn't know whether it was true, but he wanted to believe it. Everyone needs a role model, and hermits have all too few role models. Of course, Alvin was a hermit role model regardless. It's just that this story gave him a little more juice.

At any rate, our hermit-to-be was taken out to the Australian desert, where Alvin Loner lived. Alvin didn't normally accept apprentices, but our hermit-to-be was such a promising student that Alvin couldn't turn down the opportunity to work with him. They stayed there, hermiting together for a year. That was the standard length of a hermit apprenticeship.

Alvin taught our hermit-to-be all his techniques: how to maintain his focus, how not to think about women when the hormones were surging (they taught the subject extensively in school, but you had to be out in the field to be shown how to actually put it into practice), how to tell the difference between reality and hallucinations (an especially important skill when you're looking at a cobra who's about to strike, and you're not sure whether he's really there or just a figment of your imagination because you're going nuts over lack of human contact).

The two even played Chinese checkers from time to time.

At the end of the year, our hermit-to-be had not only learned a lot from Alvin, he felt inspired. He felt there was nothing he couldn't do regarding life as a hermit. Someday, maybe, he could himself be acknowledged as one of the grand masters of hermithood. He might even contribute his own articles to *Modern Hermit*.

Our hermit-to-be returned to the school with an

excellent evaluation from Alvin Loner in hand. The school officials were extremely impressed. "You're one of the best students we've ever had," they told him. "You should be able to make an impressive career as a hermit for yourself."

"Thank you. I worked very hard."

There was no graduation ceremony, of course, because that would mean getting a crowd of people together and socializing. The school gave certificates to the graduates in private and made arrangements for each of them to have a place to go live as a hermit.

It took about six more months for the school to find him a place, and the hermit-to-be continued his job as a flute teacher while he waited. Then, finally, the school contacted him. They had found him a nice, out-of-the-way spot on a mountainside, out in the middle of nowhere.

His career as a hermit was about to begin.

His friends threw him a party the night before he left. Clearly, a wild party was the opposite of the way of life he sought. But since it was just the one time and his friends wanted to do it, he could go along with it. A nice young lady went so far as to give him a personal send-off on his last night in society.

He had to get up early the next morning. His plane left at five a.m. When it landed, a private driver picked him up and took him far out into the wilderness. They drove as far as the road would take them, and then the driver stopped. "We have to walk from here," he said.

The driver led him deeper into the forest on foot. After hiking for a couple hours, they came to a fluorescent pink stake sticking up out of the ground, about four feet high, in the middle of a small clearing. A hand-painted sign with the hermit's name on it was attached. "This is it," the guide said. "This is where you'll live as a hermit."

The hermit looked around. He nodded. "Looks good," he said. "How soon can I get phone service?"

The guide looked at him blankly.

"Just kidding," the hermit said, chucking the driver on the arm. He glanced around again and added, "I know it takes about a week, probably a little longer out here."

"Are you sure you want to do this?" the driver asked.

"Just kidding," the hermit said. "Really. But, you know, it would be nice if I could get hooked up with running water. There's a limit to how primitively one should be expected to live, don't you agree?"

"I don't think you're ready for this," the driver said.

"I'm sorry," the hermit said. "I'm just nervous. This is a big day for me."

The driver seemed satisfied. He gestured around the area with a wide, generous sweep of his arm that might have made an onlooker think he was proudly showing off his estate, if an estate had been there. "Does it look okay?"

"If I say no, do I get a different place?"

"Well, no. This is it, like it or not."

"Then it looks pretty good."

They made the hike back to the car and unloaded all the hermit's stuff. He wasn't allowed to bring much with him, but when you're talking about moving someplace for the rest of your life, "not much" can still be a pretty good-sized pile of stuff. He had a few changes of clothes, the books and notebooks we mentioned earlier, some tools he could use to build his shack, and enough food (he hoped) to last until he could start living off of what he was able to grow and catch out there in the forest.

"Before I go, is there anything you'd like to say? Any messages you'd like me to take back to anyone?"

The hermit thought. He had already said pretty much everything he had wanted to say, which wasn't much to begin with. But he also felt he shouldn't pass up the opportunity. He thought about it. What to say?

After a moment, the driver said, "I take it you don't have anything to say?"

"Yes," the hermit said, "I do. I'm just thinking about how to say it."

"Well, hurry up. I have to get back to the airport and meet another new hermit."

"Okay," the hermit said, "okay, I know. Here's what I want to say: a skeleton walked into a bar and said, 'Give me a beer and a mop.'"

The driver blinked. "I've heard that one before."

"I didn't know there were requirements about it."

"Well, no, I guess not. Who do you want me to give the message to?"

"When you go back to the airport, look for a blonde woman in a red dress and tell her."

"How will I know it's the right one? I need a name or a more detailed description."

"It doesn't matter. Any blonde woman in a red dress will do."

The driver left, thinking that it was a good thing this hermit was leaving society.

It took three days for the hermit to move all his stuff from the drop-off point to his site. Remember, it was a two-hour hike from one place to the other, and when he was loaded down with stuff, it took even longer. Plus, he had to rest in between trips. Also plus, he got lost the first couple trips back to the drop-off point because there was no path. But he managed to get everything to his site.

Then it rained the first night. In addition to getting wet, the hermit was exhausted and sore and miserable. He pulled a blanket up over himself and fell asleep in the early morning hours.

Spending the night out in the open, in the rain, spurred him on to get his shack built as quickly as possible. He chopped down some trees and built himself a nice little one-room shack the way they had taught him at hermit school. He had gotten a B in the shack-making class, but this (if he said so himself) was a grade-A, prime shack. It had two closets and some shelves. It had a fireplace. It was a shack among shacks, suitable for entertaining the president of the United States if the need were to arise. But, of course, hermits don't do any entertaining. Why would the president want to visit a hermit, anyway?

It was over two months before the hermit was fully settled in. He gradually developed a schedule of eating, sleeping, meditating, writing in his journal, tending to his garden, maintaining his shack, walking about the area, daydreaming about being a rock star, and so on.

He started out on the first step to spiritual awareness, The Daisy-Lined Forest Path. It was a bright and sunny place, full of happiness and bright colors. In fact, it was much like the Bridge of Constant Focus was later to be, except that it manifested itself as—get this—a daisy-lined path through a forest.

***

Now, we've been talking about rumors throughout the story so far. We've had rumors about the mayor's daughter's behavior, we've had rumors about evil plots by both political parties, and we've had rumors about sinister threats against the poor saps who played with the mayor's daughter. All those rumors have played a big part in bringing us to the point where we are now.

So here's another rumor: from the very first days of the village, people had been spreading a rumor that an old hermit lived in a homemade shack on the mountainside. He had been seen once or twice by people who had ventured up that way to go camping or somesuch. The sightings had been only fleeting glimpses of a shaggy old man in dirty, worn-out clothes, and the sighters had just assumed he must be living somewhere on the mountain because no one had ever seen anyone who looked like that in the village.

The mayor's daughter had been insulated from many of the rumors we've seen flying about the village in the story so far, but by golly, she was well aware of this hermit rumor.

And she started thinking. If the village was dried up, she would have to start looking for playmates somewhere else, in a place where they wouldn't know about the danger involved. And, well, the only person she could think of who fit that description was the hermit—if indeed a hermit was really living up on the mountainside.

On the one hand, she had to allow as how a gruff, wrinkled, unwashed old man in worn-out clothes wasn't exactly her type.

But on the other hand, he might not be all that bad. Gruff might be sexy if he did it the right way. And the wrinkles might add character to his face, if she could see him up close. And he probably hadn't played bouncy-bouncy in oh-so-many years. He was surely overdue. He would have all sorts of excess hormones coursing through his body, probably seeping out through his pores as he slept. So he would surely be willing to get cleaned up a little bit if it meant an opportunity to play with a lovely young lady, right?

No doubt about it, she thought.

Now, don't get the wrong idea about the mayor's daughter. She didn't want to expose the hermit to the danger of getting beaten and locked up. The mere idea would horrify her. It's just that she believed that up there on the mountainside, away from the village, no one would know.

She planned her little expedition for Saturday, when she was off from work and would be able to make a day of it. By way of preparation, she got her backpack out and stuffed some food into it, along with a canteen full of water, a first-aid kit in case of snakebite, and a compass in case she got lost.

What if the hermit really didn't exist? Oh, pish-posh. He had to. He *had* to.

Saturday came, and the mayor's daughter set out on her mission. Now, understand that she didn't get out into nature very much. Okay, yeah, she knew what trees were, and that the sun was supposed to be up in the sky, and she had heard birds sing before, stuff like that.

But put it all together, and put her out in it for a whole day, and it was a revelation. She had never known such a place existed. She was in awe. She wandered around, eyes wide open, mouth agape. She forgot to look for the hermit, although she surely would have noticed had she gotten a good look at him out in the open. She was just taking in all the wonders of nature.

She stopped in the early part of the afternoon and had some lunch, some freeze-dried string cheese and a processed, synthetic pear. Yum.

On into the evening, when the sun started getting low, the mayor's daughter thought she should get back to the village before it got dark. As she walked back home, it occurred to her that this search for the hermit was going to be harder than she had expected. There was a lot of territory on that mountain, lots and lots of area to cover, and she had searched only a little bit of it.

In a way, that was all right. She could think of it as a quest, or maybe as sort of a game. It might even help distract her from the frustration of not getting the bouncy-bouncy she wanted. The only concern she had was that this hermit, according to the rumor, was old, old. So who could say how much time she could afford to spend searching? An old guy would be okay if he was all she could find. But dead would be *too* old.

***

Up on the mountainside, the hermit had another dream. He dreamed he was in his shack, and someone snuck in and started smothering him with a large kitten.

He bolted upright, awake, in a panic. He was shaking and hyperventilating. After a few minutes, he had gathered his wits. He got up and found his carrot wine.

***

The mayor's daughter called her best friend on the phone. "I was up on the mountainside today," she said. "Did you know there's a lot of nature up there? It's wonderful!"

"I knew that," the best friend said. Some people don't lead such sheltered lives.

"Why didn't you tell me?"

"Well, I guess if I had known you'd like it so much, I would have. What were you doing up there?"

"Don't ask." Really. She didn't want her friend to know she had been reduced to chasing after old, unwashed hermits.

"You were doing something you don't want to talk about."

"I was just enjoying nature. That's all."

"You didn't go to that mountainside to enjoy nature. You didn't know about nature until you were already there. Why did you decide to go in the first place?"

"Uh...curiosity."

"About what?"

Okay, the friend wasn't going to let it go. The mayor's daughter was going to have to spill it. So she was just going to blurt it out, get it over with, and hope it would blow over quickly.

As if.

"I was thinking I would see whether that old hermit was really up there," the mayor's daughter said.

"The hermit?"

"Yeah, what's wrong with that? A hermit seems like

he would be an interesting kind of guy."

"Uh, huh..."

"Really. He must have all kinds of fascinating stories."

"What kind of fascinating stories would a guy like that have? Oh, wait! Oh, no. You're not thinking..."

And then there was a very strange kind of silence. Finally, the mayor's daughter broke. "I can't get any bouncy-bouncy in the village any more. People are scared."

"So you're up there looking for an old man who may not even exist?"

"He might. If he does, I know he hasn't heard about the threats against guys who play with me. And I'm pretty sure he hasn't played bouncy-bouncy in a lot of years. He's probably overdue."

"Maybe he doesn't want to," the best friend said. "If a man becomes a hermit, there's a reason why."

"Oh, don't be silly. The hormones are still there."

***

Sunday morning the mayor's party's chairman ate a leisurely breakfast, pleased with himself. The weekend had been calm so far, without any of the phenomena that would have indicated the mayor's daughter had been up to her, uh...mischief. It was the first weekend like that in, well, in a lot of weeks. She had apparently been behaving herself—whether it was voluntary or not didn't matter. What mattered was that the rumors of scandalous behavior were going to fizzle out.

Yes, things were very well under control.

***

And the mayor wasn't thinking about anything. He was just sitting in his room playing Aardvark League Ice Hockey on his computer. Yeah, aardvarks playing ice hockey. That was pretty funny.

CHAPTER NINE

The hermit decided it was time to try going back to the Seven Mischievous Elves. He had been avoiding it. He had been drinking, going for walks, writing in his hermit journal, reading, sleeping...anything he could think of to avoid meditation. Yet he understood that the longer he put it off, the harder it would be to go back.

So he was thinking, if not now, when? Dreading it as he was, he would require special preparation. He recalled a technique they had taught him in hermit school, a sort of "pre-meditative" state, that might help. After sundown, he stood on one foot, with the other raised so his legs formed a figure four. He spread his arms straight out to the sides. He hummed at a low volume, trying to find D below middle C. Finally, he found the note and settled into a gentle monotone. He thought of aardvarks playing ice hockey and blanked his mind. He found himself in a white room about the size of a typical bedroom. It was completely featureless, with no windows, no door, and no furniture. A slight glow emanated from his hands. He could sense the taste of coffee, a slightly burned Columbian, in his mouth.

That was it. He remained that way as long as he could. He didn't know how long it lasted because he had no sense of time in that state. It didn't matter, anyway. It wasn't as if he had important appointments. Or any appointments at all, for that matter.

He finally got tired of holding that position. He sat on his bed, mind blank, and assumed his usual meditative pose.

He was back in the parking lot where the Seven Mischievous Elves had started. He looked all around, up and down, and saw nothing unusual. He started walking, and after a while, the big building came into view, looming up ahead like the carcass of a dead elephant on an African veldt. Well, except that the building wasn't all decaying and stinky, the way a dead elephant would be. And, of course, the building had a basement, which very few dead elephants have.

The hermit nudged the door open and stepped inside. He saw a flash of blinding light and was disoriented for a moment. When he could see again, he was back in the white room where he had gone for his pre-meditation.

He wasn't sure what to do. He couldn't go anywhere from the room; the only alternatives were to come out of his meditative state or to sit still and wait to see whether something might happen. Well, there was no need to come out of meditation just yet. Why not give it a little time? At least no one was making fun of him.

He sat on the floor and sang softly to himself. He sang songs like "My Daddy Invented the Popcorn Popper" and "I'm Going to Get a Tattoo of the Battle of Waterloo on My Left Instep." You know, the usual standards we all know and love.

Time stretched on. The hermit continued singing the old, well-loved songs. Eventually, he became sleepy and dozed off.

***

That afternoon, Sunday afternoon, the mayor's daughter decided to make another trip up onto the mountainside. She wanted to continue searching for the hermit, and she also wanted to commune with nature some more.

She was really getting into the communing bit. Nature was just this great big, wonderful place! She had the urge to take off all her clothes and run naked across the mountainside, through the forest, among the trees and under the birds and with the deer. She considered it a moment. The cool thing would be that if she found the hermit, she would be ready for action right away.

But then again, someone else might be out in the forest, camping or hiking. She wouldn't want to run across the wrong people in a state of undress. Plus, she might not remember where she left her clothes, and it would be, like, pretty bad if she had to walk back home naked.

No matter. She was out there, in Nature, searching for the hermit. That was the main thing.

***

Just as the mayor's daughter was getting started with her day in nature, the hermit was waking up. And he was waking up in the physical world of his shack on the mountainside. There was no trace of the white room or anything else from his meditative state.

That was very strange. In hermit school they had taught him that people don't normally doze off in the middle of meditative states. But if they do—and he had experienced this himself a few times over the years—they wake up again still in the meditative state. They don't wake up to find themselves back in the physical world.

This was sort of as if someone had pulled the plug and derailed him, or something, to mix similes. Or metaphors, or whatever it was. With all the other weirdness that had been happening, maybe he shouldn't be surprised.

And thinking back, maybe he had screwed up at the Bridge of Constant Focus. See, here's the thing about that: if the name of the step has the word "Bridge" in it, maybe that's a clue that you're supposed to take the bridge all the way across. Maybe his little rafting adventure—clever though he liked to think it was—had been cheating.

It was possible to go back and repeat a step, provided you hadn't gone too far beyond it. So he thought he could go back to the Bridge of Constant Focus if he wanted. It was there that things had started going wrong.

But then again, things maybe hadn't been quite right before he did his little raft thingy. There was the sighting of the girl. And the raised drawbridge...well, that was something wrong, he was sure of it. He hadn't started the wrongness with his raft. He had merely fed into it.

Should he go back a couple of steps?

Ah, it was all too much.

***

At the outskirts of the village, a police officer on patrol sat in his car looking up at the mountainside. He was one of the officers who were friendly with the chairman of the mayor's political party, and for the second day in a row he had just seen the mayor's daughter hike out of the village and up onto the mountainside.

The chairman of the mayor's party might, just might, be interested in this. The officer flopped open his cell phone and put in a call to the chairman.

And indeed the chairman found the news interesting. "She just went right up on the mountainside, you say?"

"Yes. And yesterday she spent the whole day up there."

"Do you think she's meeting guys up there?"

"We haven't seen any of the phenomena."

"I don't know whether that means anything," the chairman said. "We might be too far away."

"Well, sir, she goes by herself. And I haven't seen any guys go up there."

"They could be sneaking around taking a different route. I'm going to call the police chief and get him to put an extra officer on patrol at the edge of the village near the mountain." The police chief wasn't one of the officers who were friendly with the chairman, so he (the chairman) would have to think of some sort of story to get another officer assigned to that area. He, the chief, didn't want to be directly involved in any of that stuff, and he didn't want to know what was going on. He felt the need to keep up appearances, to avoid the possibility of a scandal and losing his job and going to jail. He did, however, accept occasional gifts from "an unknown source" to ignore any...uh, "untoward stories" he might hear. He received gifts like a Feldstein toilet paper dispenser (one of the top bathroom accessory designers in the business, and the dispenser had state-of-the-art electronics for the ultimate in toilet paper dispensing accuracy) and one of those eyeglass holder thingies like Steve Martin's character invented in *The Jerk*. None of these gifts was extravagant enough to arouse suspicion. It was all just part of what the chief thought of as "gracious living."

That sort of arrangement was okay with the chairman, but sometimes it meant he had to go to a little extra effort to achieve his goals. Such as now.

Maybe he should make up a story about something dangerous prowling around. That way, the police chief would have to do something because it would be a matter of public safety. The party chairman could pull some strings to make sure the officer who drew that assignment would be one of his friends.

And really, the chairman *did* think he might have seen a dragon prowling around low down on the mountainside, just a little too close to the village for comfort.

***

After making the call to the police chief, the chairman called the mayor's daughter and invited her to lunch. Now, understand that the mayor's daughter had never liked the chairman. She didn't trust him. She didn't know about all his Machiavellian plots and plans—if she had, she would have liked him even less and thought him even creepier. No, she just had a bad feeling about the guy and felt a vague discomfort at the thought of being anywhere around him.

But she figured that if he wanted to talk to her, maybe he had something on his mind that she would want to know about. In that case, she could deal with him for the half hour it would take them to have lunch.

So she met the chairman at the Dancing Goldfish Cafe. (Dancing goldfish? What the heck did that mean? Who knows? But the sign out front was amusing, with a picture of a line of goldfish dressed in tuxedos doing a little tap dance.)

The chairman didn't get right to the point. He hadn't seen the mayor's daughter in person since she was a little girl, and he wanted to chat with her for a while, just to get a sense of what kind of young lady she had grown up to become. Suspicious and on her guard, but seeing no particular reason not to talk to him, the mayor's daughter told the chairman about her interests in Halley's Comet, the works of F. Scott Fitzgerald, the influence of *The Art of War* on biochemical research, and more. She told him about her job at the animal shelter and her volunteer work at the soup kitchen. The chairman already knew about it because he worked so closely with the mayor, and of course daddies can't help but talk about their kids. Also, he had had all that research done for the tall, manly guy scheme. Still, he wanted to get her version of it.

"That's some very fine work you're doing," the chairman said.

"It's just stuff I like to do," the mayor's daughter said. "You know, helping people. Helping animals."

"Making the world a better place," the chairman

offered.

The mayor's daughter didn't like to think of it that way. It sounded so...so hokey. "Maybe just a little bit better," she said.

"It does my heart good to see young people doing good work like that."

The mayor's daughter blushed. "Well," she said, "it's better than roaming the streets stealing hubcaps."

"Yes, it's better than that." The chairman sipped from his drink and sat back regarding the girl. He cleared his throat. "What else to you like to do? Do you, maybe, enjoy going for walks in the forest?" This was a calculated risk. He was tipping his hand here; he was telling her that he was onto her plans. Her reaction could go in one of two directions. The good direction was that she would decide she had better cool it and behave herself. The bad direction was that she would get all paranoid and super careful about being followed and observed and would become sneakier and more evasive, and it would become more difficult to keep tabs on her.

What he said struck the mayor's daughter like someone smacking her in the chest with a sock full of goldfish. "Why do you ask?"

"I was just thinking the other day about how nice it is up there, all full of nature and stuff. I mean, there's more nature up there on the mountainside than there is in the village. It seems to me like a place where a person might want to spend some time communing with the universe."

She felt the need to be careful here, very careful. She knew she didn't want the chairman getting too suspicious of her intentions toward the hermit. But if he knew she was going up onto the mountainside, it would make him more suspicious if she were to deny it. "It's a nice place," she said, trying her best to sound not too interested, as if (for example) he had shown her a container full of rubber washers and she were saying, "Yeah, they're rubber washers. So what? Why are you showing them to me?"

"I was thinking," the chairman said, "that I might start going for walks up there. I just wanted to get someone else's opinion about what it's like."

"It's very nice," she said. "It's very...natureful."

***

The mayor's daughter kept making her little expeditions onto the mountainside. Weekdays, she didn't have much time for it, what with her job and her volunteer work, but occasionally she managed to do a bit of walking around shortly before dark.

She didn't try to be sneaky about it. She didn't change anything she was doing. For one thing, she didn't know what she could do differently. For another, she really was just walking around, as she had told the chairman. It was her theory that if they were watching and saw that she was just walking around, they would eventually satisfy themselves that she wasn't doing anything they disapproved of.

And, she hoped, they would no longer be watching by the time she found the hermit.

***

A week passed. Friday night, the hermit had a dream.

He dreamed he went to a big wedding. He showed up at the church, and it was crowded. All the pews were full of people dressed very nicely, and they looked happy and festive for the occasion. He was wearing a tuxedo.

The priest saw the hermit walk in, and he went over and took the hermit by the arm. "Oh, thank goodness you're here. We were afraid you'd gotten cold feet. Come on, come on. We're late getting started."

The hermit wasn't sure what all that meant, but he had an uncomfortable feeling about it.

The priest hustled him down the center aisle and stood him in front of the altar, next to—of all people—the friend who had given him the hermit school ad. The friend had a big, goofy grin on his face. He gave the hermit an enthusiastic thumbs-up. "He's here," the priest announced. "We can get started now." He signaled to the organist, who launched into a grand-sounding rendition of "Here Comes the Bride."

From a small room just inside the front door, the bride appeared. She was a pretty young lady with wavy hair and a cute button nose, elbows locked with an older man who was presumably her father. As the pair walked up the aisle toward him, the hermit recognized who she was. She was the girl from the pin the tail on the goldfish game! And her father was one of the other players!

The hermit freaked out. His brain did cartwheels inside his skull. His eyes rolled back in his head and kept rolling around, doing a 360 so they were aimed forward again.

He tried to think of something to say to excuse himself, but there was nothing to say. So he just took off. He ran down the aisle, brushing by the bride and her father, and went out the door.

He ran to the mountain and up into the forest, through the trees, running as fast as he could toward his homemade shack. When he got there, he threw the door open...

...and inside was the girl. She sat at the table, on the only chair he owned, eating some of the rabbit stew he'd made earlier that day. When she heard him at the doorway, she looked up from her bowl. "Hello, honey," she said.

***

The next day, Saturday, the mayor's daughter was ready for another full day of searching, searching in the natural beauty of Mother Nature Herself.

Along about early evening, just as she was getting ready to go home, she caught a glimpse of what looked like a human figure moving among the bushes in the distance. She stepped behind a tree and peeked around it.

The figure moved about slowly, as if cautiously approaching something. It bent over, tinkered around with something on the ground, and stood up with some sort of fuzzy-looking thing in its arms. "Oh, yeah," she heard the figure say.

He made his way around the bush and walked away, along a path that came very close to the mayor's daughter's hiding place. She ducked down as he approached, and as he passed, she could hear him mumble something about "rabbit stew tonight" to himself.

She stepped back out, away from the tree, and watched him walk into the distance. Yes, that was him.

That was the hermit walking back home with his dinner.

The mayor's daughter, oh so quietly and at the greatest distance she could manage without losing sight of him, followed. After a few minutes, he came to a small, homemade-looking shack and went in.

She sat down behind a nearby bush so he wouldn't see her if he came back out. She wanted to think for a few minutes, and she didn't want him to see her until she had figured out exactly what she was going to do. She figured that if this guy hadn't played bouncy-bouncy in fifty years, he was surely about ready and it probably wouldn't matter how she approached him. But then again, if he hadn't been around anyone at all in fifty years, the wrong move on her part might scare him away altogether. So how to figure it? Be careful, at least for now.

After a while, the hermit came out carrying an iron pot. He hung the pot from a metal tripod a few yards away from the shack and sat on the ground. Then he went to work building a fire under the pot.

She watched, from behind the bush, as he cooked what was presumably rabbit stew and drank some kind of beverage from a cup that looked as if—it couldn't have been, but it sure did look as if—it were made of leaves woven together.

After the stew had cooked for a while, the hermit took the pot off the fire and carried it back into the shack. She snuck up closer and listened. She heard him chomping and smacking his lips and saying things like "Ooh, ah, good stuff," as if he hadn't had rabbit stew in quite some time. Then he let out a loud burp that sounded as if someone were popping a twelve-foot balloon in the fifteenth dimension. Why bother with table manners if you don't think anyone else is around?

The mayor's daughter waited behind the bush for a few more minutes. There were no more signs of activity. Maybe he had gotten drunk and passed out. Eventually, she heard snoring. Well, she heard something she *hoped* was snoring.

She went back home, very careful to remember where, on this great, big, wonderful, natural mountainside, the hermit's shack was.

***

"I've found him," the mayor's daughter said, hanging out with her best friend at her best friend's house. "I've found the hermit."

"Oh, really? What does he look like?"

"Well, like a hermit. I mean, what do you think? That he's going to look like Cary Grant all dressed in formal pajamas?"

"Is he old?"

"Yeah, he's old. He's an old, an old man. He's all wrinkly, and his hair is long and gray. His clothes are worn out and falling apart." Don't they have a mall up there on the mountainside? she wondered. "And I think he smells like the carcass of a dead elephant on the African veldt, but I didn't get close enough to be sure."

"Oh, how romantic. And you want to play bouncy-bouncy with him?"

"I think the wrinkles add character to his face."

"But still..."

"Well, who else is there?"

The best friend didn't have an answer to that one.

"Did you introduce yourself?" she asked.

"No. I wanted to study him a little bit. Take a look, scope out the situation, figure out a plan."

"Do you have a plan?"

"Well, no, not yet," the mayor's daughter said. "Do you have any suggestions?"

"I don't know anything about hermits."

"You know a thing or two about men, don't you? He's a man."

"See, there's the difficulty. There are lots of different types of men."

***

The chairman of the mayor's political party wanted to know what the mayor's daughter was doing up on that mountainside. It was possible that deprived of her bouncy-bouncy, she was simply substituting long walks through the forest and communing with natural wonders of Mother Nature, which were quite naturally wonderful.

It was also possible that she had some sort of clever little scheme to play bouncy-bouncy up there with someone. And if that was what she was doing, he wanted to find out before the news reporters did. He called his police officer friends and asked them to follow her up onto the mountainside and keep her under surveillance. Don't do anything; just watch her and report back.

***

The mayor's daughter, concerned about finding just the

right approach, was doing some research. She went to the library and found books about hermits and books about how to pick up men. She found a couple of psychology books that might have some useful info. She went to a used bookstore and was able to find a couple of the textbooks they used in hermit school.

And she read. And read. She did some research on the Internet. All the stuff she was learning led her to think she might just be better off if she were to give up on this zany scheme to seduce the hermit. She had gotten the impression that it wasn't going to be possible, that very likely he had reached a high level of spiritual attainment, and that things like playing bouncy-bouncy were far behind him, far in his past, of no more concern to him now than one of the dirty diapers his mother had pulled off of his little infant bottom all those years ago.

She was starting to think that she should just suck it up, so to speak, and make peace with her newfound life of celibacy. Maybe she would even become a hermit in her own fashion. She had learned enough about it.

***

It didn't go without notice that she had stopped making her trips up onto the mountainside. The chairman found this suspicious, highly suspicious. If she were just interested in nature, she wouldn't have stopped so suddenly. Clearly, she wasn't sick; she was still doing all the other stuff she normally did. Something had happened.

He had his friendly officers make a few inquiries around town. One officer found that out that the mayor's daughter had been making regular trips to the library, so he went there to talk to the librarian. "Has the mayor's daughter been in here?" he asked.

"I've seen her in here a few times," the librarian said.

"Do you know why she's coming in? What books has she checked out?"

"I'm afraid I can't tell you that," the librarian said. "That's confidential info."

"Oh, I understand," the officer said. "I understand perfectly, and I wouldn't want you to break the rules." He turned to go, but then he stopped. "It's just that..." he let the sentence trail off.

"What?" the librarian asked.

"Well, it's just that rumors about a dragon have been going around the village."

"Dragon?"

"You've heard them, I'm sure."

"No, I'm afraid I haven't."

"The rumors say there's a dragon living on the mountainside. Sometimes he prowls around at the edge of the village. They say he looks hungry."

"Oh, that's scary."

"Yeah, very scary. You know what dragons eat, don't you?"

"People?"

"Not just any people. Children. They eat children. They consider babies a special delicacy."

"Oh, no!" The librarian was horrified.

"Yeah, so we have to be very careful."

"But what does that have to do with the mayor's daughter?"

"We think she might be doing research to find out

how to slay the dragon."

"Oh, that's good."

"No, it's not," the officer said. "Slaying a dragon is no job for an amateur. You have to undergo rigorous training and work as an apprentice for five years. If you just read a book and then try to go out and slay a dragon, you won't do anything but get him mad, and that makes him hungrier."

"Oh, that will never do."

"No, it won't. It won't do at all. If he gets mad, he'll eat the mayor's daughter and then come charging into town." He paused and then added—just to pile it up a little higher—"And you know who he'll be looking for?"

The librarian thought for just a moment. "Babies?"

The officer nodded.

The librarian turned white. "That's horrible. But why don't you just ask her what she's doing and explain things to her?"

"We tried that. You may not know this, but she's a very headstrong young lady. She wouldn't tell us whether she's going to try to slay the dragon or not."

The librarian looked thoughtful, turning the story over in her head and considering whatever nuances it might have. She looked as if she wanted to ask a question but thought better of it. "I can't tell you what she's checked out, but it seems to me that if I were to go into the ladies' room for a few minutes, I can't help it if someone happens to come around behind the desk here and look it up on the computer."

"No, you couldn't help it at all," the officer said. "It just totally wouldn't be your fault. Everybody has to go to the ladies' room from time to time."

The librarian cleared her throat. "Okay, well, I have

to go visit the little girls' room. I'll be gone for a few minutes. I hope no one looks at my computer." With that, she went off to the ladies' room.

The police officer quickly went around the desk and typed a query into the computer. A list came up with all the books the mayor's daughter had recently checked out. The officer grabbed a piece of paper and wrote down the titles. He pocketed the paper and moved back around to where he was before.

The librarian came back. "Is there anything else I can do for you?" she asked.

"I don't think so. If you can't tell me what books she has, I guess I'll just have to go away without knowing."

CHAPTER TEN

The chairman looked over the mayor's daughter's reading list with interest, great interest. Books on hermits. Books on sex. Books on psychology. Further, the officer had stopped at the used bookstore and found out about the hermit school textbooks.

"I think it's pretty clear what's going on," the chairman said. "I think she's trying to overcome her physical urges, and she plans to become a hermit."

The officer chewed on that one a bit and then said, "You don't think she might be trying to figure out how to seduce that hermit up on the mountainside?"

The chairman shook his head. "Son, you got a lot to learn about women. First, no one's sure there's really a hermit up there. Why would she go to all that trouble for someone who might not exist? Second, if he's really up there, he'll be old, an old man. He'll be gruff and unwashed and wrinkly, and his hair will be long and gray. His clothes will be worn out and falling apart. He'll smell like the carcass of a dead elephant on the African veldt. Do you think for an instant she'd want to play bouncy-bouncy with someone like that?"

"She might think gruff is sexy if he does it right."

"But he's still wrinkled and unwashed."

"Well, she might think the wrinkles add character to his face. And she might think he's ready to play bouncy-bouncy after decades without it. She might think he would be willing to get cleaned up if he had a reason to."

"I don't think facial character is a big factor for her."

"But if no one else is available, she might consider it."

"No, it's just too far-fetched. I'm sure she's seen the town has dried up. There's no more bouncy-bouncy for her, so she's going to change her ways and become a hermit."

Well, okay, whatever, the officer thought. He had done his job. He had gotten the info the chairman wanted, and it wasn't his job (the officer's) to interpret the results. He made a bit of money on the side doing these little chores for the party chairman, but otherwise he had no particular reason to care what happened with the girl. Whatever she did, he was still going to get up the next day and work his shift and collect his paycheck every two weeks. So there.

The party chairman was quite enthusiastic about his new hypothesis. He felt like a real crime buster, like those guys on the TV shows who are so clever and solve all the crimes that no one else could solve with the clever use of their own cleverness. Maybe he could have his own show, where he would catch bad guys by the sheer force of his almost supernatural intuition—with the help of his sidekick Herman, who would do all the legwork.

But for now, back to the business at hand. If the mayor's daughter wanted to become a hermit, that suited him just fine. In fact, maybe he could even do a little to encourage her.

He went to the computer, found a big bookselling web site, and searched for books about being a hermit. The site had a surprisingly generous selection of titles, including four by a fella named Alvin Loner: *How to Become a Hermit for Fun and Profit*, *The Inner Hermit Within You and the Outer Hermit Without You*, *Adventures in Hermitism*, and *I'm a Hermit, You're a Hermit, We're All Hermits*. According to the customer comments, this Loner guy had apparently been some big-shot, legendary, old-school hermit years ago. The chairman figured he must have known what he was talking about. He ordered a copy of each to be sent to the mayor's daughter as a gift. He didn't want her to know he was the one who had sent them because he was sure she wouldn't trust him. She would know something funny was going on. So he had the web site include a card that said, "From Your Friend." What the heck.

***

The books arrived a few days later. The mayor's daughter was pleased, even if it was sort of puzzling for them to show up out of the blue like that. What friend had sent them? She was sure it couldn't have been her best friend because she wouldn't have sent them. Her best friend didn't want to encourage her to do anything with the hermit. And if she *had* sent them, she would have put "best friend" on the card.

The mayor's daughter had other friends, of course. It's just that she didn't think any of them would spend the money to send her so many books for no apparent reason. Some of them might send her one book, maybe. Four? That's a lot, all at once. She didn't even think anyone else knew that hermits held any special interest for her in any way—unless her best friend had spilled, but she wouldn't. Well, she (the mayor's daughter) would figure it out. Maybe someone would say something about it.

Another thing about this package of hermit books showing up at her house—all written by this Alvin Loner dude, who seemed to be some sort of big-time, A-list, legendary hermit Back in the Day, according to the Internet, so he must have known what he was talking about—was that they came at a particularly good time. This notion that she should give up on her plan to seduce the hermit had been getting stronger in her mind. Every time she thought about it, it made just a little more sense.

So what did the appearance of all these books mean?

It occurred to her...no, it was too crazy to be true... but still, crazier things had happened...no, she couldn't believe it...but why not? It occurred to her that the hermit, the old guy on the mountainside, could have found out that she had her sights set on him, and that she wasn't sure how to approach him. Maybe it had come to him in some sort of meditative vision or something.

Maybe he had sent the books. Maybe he wanted her to come to him, possibly so that they could live as hermits together, and this was his way of encouraging her.

Unlikely. Highly unlikely. Yet she couldn't think of any explanation that was *more* likely.

***

On the mountainside, the hermit was all discombobulated. In case you're wondering, discombobulation is a little bit worse than bewilderment, but not as bad as befuddlement. I think.

Anyway, what was going on with the hermit was that he had been trying to get back into his meditative state, but he just couldn't. He was going to try to go back a couple steps and retrace his path to see whether he had done something wrong. It was no use, though. He couldn't get in. He had tried to go into his "pre-meditative" state that he had used before, but he couldn't even achieve that.

Maybe he was trying too hard. He was beginning to think that he was going to have to give up—just for a while, so he could mellow out a bit and get himself re-energized, back on the right track.

And yet the dreams continued. They didn't come every night, but he'd had a couple more, following up on the one in which he had apparently been married to the cute girl with wavy hair. There was one in which she had cleaned the place up and bought furniture—nice stuff, matching pieces, no less—and silverware, all the stuff you'd want to set up house. She even had carpeting installed. In a homemade shack, mind you! She just didn't get it.

In another, her mother came to visit.

He was getting afraid to fall asleep. But if he didn't, his problems would only get worse. Sleep deprivation can have pretty nasty effects.

***

While all this was going on, the mayor was blissfully

oblivious of everything. There was no evidence that his daughter had been misbehaving lately—she had been spending all her time reading—and the party chairman wasn't getting on his case about keeping her under control. So he was happy.

***

Okay, this was it. This was the big day. It was Saturday, and the mayor's daughter had cleared her social calendar and written down just one event: she was going to go up on the mountainside, find the hermit, and seduce him.

But first, she had to prepare. She started by going to the village's high-end women's apparel store. She shopped and looked around and shopped some more. She had a lot of money to spend, and she was serious about looking good.

"I want to make the best possible impression on a man," she told the saleslady. "I want something that's at the height of village fashion. I want something that's stunning yet subtle, that's sophisticated yet naive, that's green yet orange. Can you fix me up?"

"I have just the thing," the saleslady gushed. She had an inkling that the mayor's daughter had some kind of misbehavior on tap, and she didn't approve, but she gushed anyway. They all gush if you're going to spend a lot of money. She found just the right outfit for the mayor's daughter, an outfit I won't describe because you can imagine something much better than anything I can put down in words.

The mayor's daughter tried it on, and she was highly impressed. "It's lovely," she gushed. "Simply lovely."

She looked at herself in the mirror, turning and posing like a contestant on one of those fashion model reality shows on TV.

Then she went to the perfume department. "I want a fragrance that's distinctive yet unassuming, strong yet delicate, and musky yet flowery. What can you do for me?"

"I have just the thing," the saleslady said. She sprayed a spritz of Sportive on a sponge and held it out for the mayor's daughter to sniff.

"Oh, yes, that's just what I'm looking for."

Her next stop was the hair salon. "I want something that's at the height of village fashion," she said. "I want something that's fancy yet simple, that's high-class yet ordinary, that's long yet short."

The hair stylist thumbed through a few hairstyle magazines for inspiration. "Okay," she said," I know just what to do." She went to work.

Then to the manicurist. "I want a manicure," she said.

An hour later, the mayor's daughter came out with just the right hairstyle and nails.

She went home and slathered on some makeup. She put on her new outfit and examined herself in the mirror, doing some more of those contestant-on-fashion-model-reality-show poses.

The mayor's daughter was satisfied with her appearance. She was going to impress the pants off of that old hermit up there on the mountainside. Literally.

***

The hermit was just finishing up dinner when the mayor's daughter approached him. Nice day that it was, he was outside sitting on a tree stump, table brought outside and placed in front of him, so he could enjoy the sunshine as he dined.

She came into the clearing acting as if she belonged there. "Hi," she said. "How are you?"

"Beg pardon?" the hermit said. He looked up and saw a cute girl with wavy hair and a button nose. He saw the girl who had played pin the tail on the goldfish and made fun of him. He saw the girl he had been married to in those awful dreams. For a moment, one terrible, horribly bad moment, he felt the tree stump dissolve from under him. The ground dissolved. The rest of the world dissolved. He was left in free fall, drifting through a solid gray mass of nothingness.

The girl stepped closer. "How are you?"

"Who are you?"

"I'm the mayor's daughter." She held out her hand. He regarded it for a moment and gave her a weak, insincere handshake.

She looked at his face. He looked pretty good for an old man. He had leathery skin and some wrinkles, but the years hadn't beaten up on him nearly as much as she might have expected. (Was it possible that a life of spirituality and eating food without preservatives was, like, actually good for you?) And also, he looked as if, once upon a time, he had probably been a fairly dashing and handsome young man.

"Mayor? Of what?"

"My daddy's the mayor of that little village down at the foot of the mountain."

"What are you doing here?"

"I wanted to come up here and meet you."

"Meet me?"

"Sure. Down in the village, we have these rumors about a hermit living up on the mountainside. I wanted to see whether you were really here."

"I'm here. Are you satisfied?"

She stepped closer. "It's going to take a little more than that to satisfy me."

"I'm sorry, but that's the best I can do for you."

She eyed the tree stump. "Can I sit down?"

"To tell the truth, I'd rather be alone," the hermit said. "That's why I became a hermit." Also, after all the dreams and messed-up meditation sessions, he kinda didn't trust her.

The mayor's daughter looked as if her feelings were hurt. "I fixed myself up real pretty, and came all the way up here just to see you, and you haul off and tell me to go away? The least you could do is talk to me for a few minutes."

"Well, I appreciate the effort, but..."

"Don't you think I look pretty?"

After fifty years of hermithood, the hermit wasn't sure what pretty was anymore. She sure was nice to look at, though. "You're very pretty."

She smiled and took another step closer. "Now we're getting somewhere."

"I would really like to go back to being a hermit," he said.

The mayor's daughter moved to sit down, although there was no room on the tree stump for her. She bumped his hip with hers, trying to get him to scoot over. "Can I sit down?"

"Not to be antisocial, but I'd rather you didn't."

"Oh, come on." She bumped again. "How long has it been since you talked to someone? Had a nice conversation about your hopes and dreams for the future, and stuff?" This was more difficult than she had expected, believing as she did that he had sent those books as a way to encourage her. But his social skills had probably atrophied after all those years of being alone. If she had patience, he would catch on.

"I'm seventy and live alone in a forest. What do you think my hopes and dreams for the future are?"

"You're gruff, but I like it," she said. "Wouldn't you like to talk to someone about books, or politics, or green peppers, or...*anything*?"

"You're very persistent, aren't you?"

"I'm a force of nature." She smiled a big, toothy smile. A photographer could have used her teeth to reflect light. "Do you want to tell me about yourself?" She nudged again.

And the invitation to talk about himself was all it took. The hermit scooted over to make room for the mayor's daughter. He still didn't trust her, though.

"I think hermits are fascinating," she said. "How did you become a hermit?"

"You really want to know?"

"I've been reading about hermits." She leaned in closer, and her voice took on a more meaningful tone. "I've been reading books by Alvin Loner."

"Alvin Loner?" Ah, that brought back memories. They had had some good times, he and Alvin Loner, during his apprenticeship. They had...well, they had done some stuff...well, actually, he couldn't remember it very well at all. To be truthful, he seemed to remember that Loner had been something of a jerk. Okay, not "something of," but a real, total, full-blown, certified, official jerk. He had insisted the hermit-to-be scrub his floor clean. Hey, it was a *dirt floor*. How the heck do you scrub dirt clean? To give him his due, though, Alvin Loner did know everything there was to know about being a hermit.

"Oh, yes. His books are very interesting," the mayor's daughter said.

"I think they are."

"Alvin Loner has given me a whole new appreciation of what it means to be a hermit."

The hermit had an impulse to ask why, if the girl appreciated hermithood so much, she was so intent upon forcing her company upon him. On the other hand, she knew all about Alvin Loner, and that counted for something.

Also, it was kind of pleasant to sit there with her, even though he didn't want to think about that.

So the hermit told the mayor's daughter his life story, about his habit of hiding from everyone throughout his childhood, and so on. He told her about hermit school and his apprenticeship with Alvin Loner. He told her about coming to live on the mountainside.

"That's fascinating," she said.

"Yes, well, if you don't mind, I need to meditate now." He wasn't really going to meditate; he was still taking some time off. He hadn't told her anything about the dreams or the meditations that had gone bad.

The mayor's daughter wanted to push just a little further, to say something like, "I'm sure you need to relax...maybe I could help..." or something equally suggestive. She didn't, though. She thought the best thing was probably to let it rest for the time being. She knew where to find him. She could come back.

And as she walked back home, a police officer friendly to the party chairman watched from a distance. As soon as she was far enough away not to hear him, he whipped out his cell phone.

***

"Ah," the party chairman said. "She found the old hermit up there. Very interesting. What did they do?"

"They talked."

"Just talked?"

"That's right, sir. They just talked. She didn't make a move to kiss him or anything. Both of them kept their hands to themselves. She was all fixed up real pretty looking, like to make a good impression, but all they did was talk."

"I guess I understand why she would go to some effort to look pretty," the chairman said. "She obviously wanted to make a good impression so he would give her advice on becoming a hermit."

"That's what it looked like."

"Okay, good work. I think we can lay this one to rest. I think the mayor's daughter is going to behave herself from now on."

***

At the soup kitchen, the mayor's daughter was telling her best friend about her latest adventure. "I had a nice little visit with the hermit," she said. "I talked to him."

"Talked? Is that all?"

"Yeah, is that all?" A man held his plate out. The

mayor's daughter blopped a blop of candied sparrow kidneys on his plate. (If you think candied sparrow kidneys sound disgusting, the point is that they're nutritious and cheap, making them a favorite choice for soup kitchen menu makers.)

"That's all," the mayor's daughter said. "He's a nice guy. I had a good time."

"So you want to be just friends with him, nothing else?"

"I didn't have *that* good a time."

"Do you think he really wants to play bouncy-bouncy with you? Think about it. Why do you think he became a hermit?"

"Well, gee, he became a hermit fifty years ago. A lot can change in fifty years." The mayor's daughter just couldn't understand the notion that playing bouncy-bouncy might not be at the top of everyone's list of priorities. (It's not something I understand, either, but I know it happens.)

"But if he changed his mind and decided he wanted to play bouncy-bouncy, don't you think he'd just give up being a hermit and go find himself a girlfriend?"

"I don't know what he would do. But I *do* think he wants to play bouncy-bouncy. He just doesn't know it yet."

***

The hermit was what they call cautiously optimistic. A few days had passed, the girl hadn't come back, and he hadn't had any more of those tormenting dreams.

Were things returning to normal?

Maybe now was the time to try meditating again.

He had decided that his plan would be to backtrack to Step 134, The Golden Wolf and the Beginning of Destiny. That would take him through the Bridge of Constant Focus again, which should be much easier this time if nothing went wrong, which would in turn give him a running start at tackling the Seven Mischievous Elves.

Yeah, that would be good.

He went into his pre-meditative state and found himself in the white room again. So far, so good. He remained there for a while, savoring the atmosphere of the place—inasmuch as one can savor the atmosphere of a place that doesn't have any atmosphere and doesn't really exist.

After a while he came back out, oh so gently. He sat on his bed enjoying the aftereffect, which was a sort of feeling like an electrical backwash running through the shack. As the aftereffect subsided, he took his position for actual meditation.

The hermit concentrated on his breathing, which had always been the weak point in his meditation technique. In hermit school, his instructors had been concerned about his ability to breathe properly for the best results. They had given him individual instruction and assigned him special breathing exercises. Even with all the extra work, he passed the course with the disappointing grade of D.

Now he was careful to make sure he got it right. He didn't want to leave anything to chance.

It was slow, but the meditative state gradually came. The hermit was at the entrance to a tunnel, a long, dark tunnel at the foot of a mountain.

This was as it had been the first time through. The

hermit stepped into the tunnel. A bit of moonlight seeped into the entrance, and then, after a few steps, he was in total darkness. Again, this was the way it had been the first time. He walked slowly, hands out in front of him to feel for the walls. He knew the tunnel would twist around considerably as he went deeper.

About two hours in, he could see a dim glow coming from something around a bend in the tunnel. He made his way around the bend and came to a radiant golden statue of a wolf. Its pose was mid-stride while running, legs extended, tail whooshing back. Its mouth was open.

The hermit reached into the wolf's mouth, felt around, and pulled out a key. He smiled. Yes, all was going well.

He continued along the tunnel, past the glow and into the total darkness again, carefully feeling his way along.

From up ahead, off in the distance, the hermit could hear the faint sound of chanting. That wasn't part of this step. Maybe it was a variation, though. He wasn't sure whether he should expect everything to be identical to the way it had been the first time. As he understood it, it was extremely rare for anyone to backtrack and repeat steps. Even the experts—even Alvin Loner—might not understand how it worked.

The chanting got louder, and the hermit finally came to a chamber that was lit with fluorescent tubes mounted on the ceiling.

Dozens of little goldfish were all over the floor, upright on their tail fins, dancing and chanting something that sounded like a football cheer. The girl goldfish were wearing wigs of wavy black hair. One of the goldfish saw the hermit and stopped. “Look! There he is!” he shouted. The rest of them stopped dancing and started laughing at him. They were rolling on the floor.

This wasn’t right.

The hermit also saw that the chamber was a cul-de-sac. There was no way forward. The first time through, he had reached the other end of the tunnel without anything untoward happening. A door had there, which he had unlocked with the key from the wolf's mouth. Then out into the forest, where he had done some other stuff.

There had been no dancing fish, that was for darned sure.

***

Saturday rolled around again, and the mayor’s daughter got fixed up real pretty. She was going up to the mountainside to visit the hermit, and she was going to close the deal. She was going to seduce him this time.

Yes, today was the day it was going to happen.

The police officers who were friendly with the chairman saw her walk up into the forest, but they didn’t pay attention. The chairman, convinced that she was getting advice from the old man about how to become a hermit, no longer needed reports on her movements.

She reached the shack and knocked on the door. No answer. She nudged the door open, just a little bit, and peeped inside. He wasn’t home.

That was okay; she could wait. She stepped inside and looked around. Nice place, for a homemade shack that was built fifty years ago on a mountainside by a guy who had marginal carpentry skills—“marginal” being a good word if you expand its definition to include incompetence.

She found his books and looked through them. He had an impressive library, if you're impressed by lots of books on hermithood. She selected *The Thirteen Secrets of a Master Hermit* by Horace Solo and sat down on the bed to read.

Two hours later she was about a hundred pages in, deep into the intricacies of the fifth secret, when the door opened and the hermit appeared. She looked up from the book. "Hi," she said. "I've been waiting for you."

"What are you doing here?"

"That's not a friendly way to greet someone."

The hermit turned petulant. "I'm a hermit. I'm not supposed to be friendly."

"Well, you're not supposed to be mean, either."

He stood in the doorway regarding her for several moments and then went to the table and sat down. "Look," he said, "it was pleasant talking to you that one time, but you need to understand that it was just one time. If you've been studying up on hermits, you should know that. If you start coming up here all the time, I won't be a hermit any longer."

"Maybe there are more important things," the mayor's daughter said.

"You don't get to decide what's important to me."

"Can I be your apprentice?"

"You have to go to hermit school first."

She stood and walked around the table. "Oh, piffle. No one has to know." She stopped behind him and started massaging his shoulders. It felt nice, he had to admit. She had strong fingers that seemed to find just the right place and apply just the right pressure. He sighed and closed his eyes.

"Do you like that?" she asked.

"It feels good."

"Does that mean you don't want me to leave?"

"That means…" The hermit stopped short. What *did* it mean?

Her hands edged their way into his shirt, through the loose neck opening. She began caressing his chest lightly. He took her wrists in a firm grasp. "I don't think you should do that," he said.

"Why? Are you married?"

"What kind of silly question is that?"

"Well, what other objection could you possibly have? We're both adults. No one's getting hurt."

The hermit stood up and moved around so the table was between them. "You're missing the point," he said. "This kind of thing is just not what I do. You don't call an electrician if you need a plumber."

"That doesn't make sense. I don't need an electrician or a plumber. I need a manly, virile hermit, and I've found one."

"I'm not as virile as you might think."

She stepped around the table and put her arms around him. "I'll be the judge of that."

He pushed her away. "No, I don't think it would work."

"Why? Do you prefer men?"

"No, I don't prefer men. I'm just saying, my chosen way of life is to be by myself."

"Oh, come on. Everyone has…needs. How long has it been since you've played bouncy-bouncy?"

"It doesn't matter."

"I don't think you believe that any more than I do,"

the mayor's daughter said. "You're a healthy man, right?"

"I don't know. I haven't been to the doctor in fifty years."

"Have you played bouncy-bouncy since you've been a hermit?"

The hermit sighed impatiently. It was a very forceful kind of sigh, a sigh that could have driven a railroad spike into a granite wall. It was a good thing he aimed it down at the floor. "No, I haven't," he said.

"All that time," the mayor's daughter said, in a sort of faraway tone that sounded as if she were musing to herself. "All those years and years without any women around. It must have been tough."

The hermit sat down on the bed, just because he was tired of standing. "It's tough at first, but over the years it gets easier."

The mayor's daughter sat next to him. Her hand found its way to his knee. "You've been missing out," she said. "What would it hurt to get into a little bouncy-bouncy with a hot young babe who admires you? After it's over, I could go home and you could go back to being a hermit, and we would both be happy."

"Why do you want to do this?" the hermit asked. "Do you have a bet with someone that you can seduce the crazy old hermit up on the mountainside? Are you trying to win some money?"

She recoiled. "No! How could you say such a thing? I think my sincerity is plain to be seen."

"I was just thinking, girls get to talking about things; maybe it would be a challenge."

"No, I'm not doing this as a challenge. I'm doing this because it's what I want to do."

"Well, I hate to disappoint you because you seem like such a nice girl and all, but it's not what I want to do."

"You're not going to budge, are you?"

"No, I'm sorry. I don't think I am."

She leaned over and gave him a quick peck on the cheek. "You think about it. I'll come back again, and you can tell me if you change your mind."

CHAPTER ELEVEN

Here's the deal: The hermit had, as he told the mayor's daughter, put thoughts of women behind him. He had put those thoughts behind him long ago. But now, the mayor's daughter had rekindled those thoughts. Once again, he was thinking about women. And he didn't want to be doing that because no matter how nifty women might be, he wanted more than anything else to be a good hermit.

He had put his whole life into it.

Maybe, just maybe, if she hadn't said she would come back, he could go back to the way he was before. Maybe he could forget about this whole incident, the shoulder massage (oh, it was nice, to be sure), her attempted seduction.

But if she was going to come back, it wasn't over. He would have to prepare himself, figure out some kind of defensive strategy or something. Otherwise, she might just wear him down.

They hadn't taught him about this at hermit school. No one had anticipated that a pretty young lady might be intent upon seducing a hermit, intent upon seducing him the way a cat is intent upon attacking the poor, scared mouse he's cornered.

The hermit didn't want to think about it that way. Let's just say the mayor's daughter was intent upon seducing him the way an aardvark is intent upon being the first word in the dictionary.

No, that doesn't even make sense. He didn't know what it was like. What he *did* know, however, that he had no doubt that the mayor's daughter was going to make good on her threat to come back, and he had to figure out some way to fend her off.

***

That night, a shadowy figure—a mysterious stranger—showed up at the hermit's shack. He knocked on the door and walked right in just as the hermit was relaxing in bed, about to fall asleep.

"Hello, hermit," the mysterious stranger said.

"Oh, no, not another visitor. I hope I'm not getting popular," the hermit said. "That would be kind of like the opposite of being a hermit."

"Don't think for an instant that I'm here because I enjoy your company," the mysterious stranger said.

"Oh, no. Never. But who are you?"

The mysterious stranger paused for effect. He walked around in the shack, looking the place over as if he were considering buying it. "Not bad," he said. "Did you build this place yourself?"

"Uh, yeah. But who are you?"

The mysterious stranger pulled the chair around next to the bed and sat down. "I'm a mysterious stranger, come to torment you."

"Stand in line, buddy."

"In line behind the mayor's daughter? Well, that's

what I've come to talk about."

The hermit bolted upright in bed, gauging how big and mean this "mysterious stranger" guy was and noting (with some alarm) that he had positioned himself between the hermit and the door. "I didn't touch her," the hermit said. "We just talked. That's all."

The mysterious stranger laughed. "No, that's not it. I'm not here to defend her honor." He leaned closer. "In fact, if you *had* touched her—I mean, like *touched* her—I probably wouldn't be here."

The hermit relaxed a bit, but he still wasn't ready to believe this guy was okay. "I'm afraid I don't follow."

The mysterious stranger sat back and lit a cigarette. He puffed slowly, giving his full attention to the smoke. The hermit watched. The smoke had a full, rich fragrance, not entirely unpleasant. Maybe it was some sort of expensive, exotic blend. "You don't mind if I smoke, do you?"

In fact, the hermit did mind. But the mysterious stranger had already started, so what the heck. Besides, if he got the place all full of cigarette smoke, maybe that would be a turn-off for the mayor's daughter. "Go ahead," the hermit said.

The mysterious stranger took a couple more hits off the cigarette, slowly, making a point of showing his enjoyment. The hermit wanted to get the conversation over and done with so this guy would go the heck away, but apparently it was not to be.

"It's like this," the mysterious stranger finally said. "You know the mayor's daughter has her eye on you."

"And the rest of her, too, if she had her way."

"Yeah. That's just the point. You should."

"I should? What do you know about all this, anyway?

Did she send you here?"

"Oh, no. No, she didn't. No one in the village has any interest in trying to get you two together. Even her own best friend thinks it's a misguided idea."

"I get it. You're just a figment of my imagination. I'm dreaming you."

"If that's the way you want to think about it, okay. It doesn't matter. I'm just coming here to offer you some food for thought. I hope you think about it, but the bottom line is that you should do whatever you want."

"Okay, then, what's the food for thought?"

"Go for it, man. Go for it. You owe it to yourself. You've been out here in the middle of nowhere for most of your life. You've been a good hermit."

"A daggone good hermit."

"Yes, a daggone good hermit. You deserve a little reward for all those years of being a good hermit."

"But being a good hermit is its own reward."

The mysterious stranger fixed a "you can't be serious" gaze on the hermit. It was a very strong gaze, so strong it actually pushed the hermit back a couple inches. "You deserve to indulge yourself, just a little bit," the mysterious stranger said.

"But it's against the whole concept of being a hermit."

"So what? You knock one out and then go back to your hermit ways. Think of it as being on a diet. Someone loses a bunch of weight and feels good. It doesn't matter if they have just one little piece of cake, maybe a piece of rich chocolate cake with oh-so-thick icing, as a reward for their hard work, does it?"

"It's not like that," the hermit said. "I'm not sure it would stop at just one time."

The mysterious stranger got up and paced about the room, deep in thought. He suddenly wheeled around to face the hermit and pointed at his face. "Where were you on the evening of July fifteenth?" he demanded.

"What?"

"Sorry. I always wanted to do that." He sat down again. "What I'm saying is, you live in the physical world here, right? That means you have to...well, live in the physical world."

"I've done all right so far as a hermit. That is, until that girl showed up."

"Done all right?" The mysterious stranger looked around the shack. "You call this..." He swept his hands around to indicate their surroundings. "...doing all right?" Something caught his attention. Distracted, he walked over to the corner, where the hermit's coat was hanging from a peg on the wall. He took the coat down and held it at arm's length. "This thing is *hideous*!"

"So what?"

"So nothing. Never mind the coat, if that's what it's supposed to be. I'm just saying indulge yourself. It'll do you good."

"I'm going to go ahead and disagree with that."

"Look, man," the mysterious stranger said, "what do you think that thing down there is for?"

"What thing?"

"That thing that hangs down in front of you. You have it because you were meant to use it. Nothing wrong with that. It's natural."

"I've used it. I used it before I became a hermit."

"Fifty years ago. Look, man, this spiritual stuff is all well and good. It's okay to make it the focus of your life if you want. But you're going too far. There's no reason to deny yourself a little pleasure. You need to have a little more balance in your life."

"I need to have fewer people in my life," the hermit said. He lay down and pulled his blanket over his head.

The mysterious stranger rose. "It makes no difference to me what you do," he said. "I just hate to see someone get too wrapped up in one particular thing to enjoy what there is to be enjoyed in life."

The hermit pulled the blanket tighter around himself.

"Just think about it," the mysterious stranger said.

"Just think about biting my rear end," the hermit said through his blanket.

***

For the next few days, the mayor's daughter spent all her free time reading about hermits. In particular, she delved very deeply into her Alvin Loner books. She thought she might get some important personal insights from those books because, of course, her hermit on the mountainside had served his apprenticeship with him.

That Alvin Loner, she thought, I bet he was pretty hot. And here she was...she knew someone who had actually known him.

One night she took a little break from her reading to call her best friend. "I made my move," the mayor's daughter said.

"Your move?"

"I tried to seduce the hermit."

"How did it go?"

"About the way I expected. He resisted."

"So you didn't score," the best friend said.

"No, not yet. But he's thinking about it. I'm sure he must be thinking about it."

"If he doesn't want to play bouncy-bouncy, why don't you just leave him alone?"

"Because I think that after he gives in, he'll be glad he did."

"No. After he gives in, *you'll* be glad he did."

"What do you know about it? You've never seduced a hermit."

***

Meanwhile, the hermit was contemplating what to do about his meditation problems. No matter what he tried, something was messed up in some way, somehow. It defied explanation, although that mayor's daughter girl was clearly mixed up in it some way. He didn't know whether she was deliberately trying to throw him off the path for some reason, or if his meditation problems were an unintended result of her wanting to play bouncy-bouncy with him. Which was it? If he could answer that question, it might give him a clue as to how to solve the problem.

Unfortunately, he had no idea how to answer the question. He didn't know where to start. If he were to ask her, he couldn't assume she would tell him the truth.

He went into his meditative state a couple more times in the next few days, but each time he landed back at the chamber with the dancing goldfish. It was amusing, he thought. They had some nice choreography, no doubt. Yet there was no way out of the chamber except to go back the way he had come in.

So the hermit wasn't able to make any progress. What made it worse was the mayor's daughter coming in and making moves on him—not just that she was showing up in visions and dreams and whatnot, but that she had shown up in person. That was really throwing things out of whack for him. She was going to come back. She had said so, and he was sure she meant it, and he didn't know what he would do when she showed up again.

He had resisted, but she was probably going to be more forceful about it next time.

And just who the heck was this mysterious stranger guy, anyway, waltzing into his shack like some kind of mysterious stranger kind of guy who thinks he knows everything and telling the hermit he should go for it? Where did he come off doing that? Who did he think he was?

The hermit tried to distract himself. He took long walks. He talked to the trees (no, they didn't talk back). He sang songs. He drank. He started carving little sculptures of sticks of chewing gum out of twigs. He tried growing new things in his garden, things like rutabagas and radishes and tofu. He didn't have much luck with the tofu. All that stuff worked for a while—to distract him, that is—but his mind always drifted back to the mayor's daughter.

Yes, the urge to play bouncy-bouncy is a strong one indeed. That thing the mysterious stranger had mentioned, that thing the hermit had hanging down in front of him, well…it was starting to behave like something that wasn't hanging down anymore. It was getting interested in this whole idea, all on its own.

This was bad, the hermit thought. This was very bad. He kept thinking about how bad it was as he drew water up from his well to get all washed up. He kept thinking about how bad it was as he combed the leaves and twigs out of his tangled-up hair and beard. He kept thinking about how bad it was as he wondered whether chewing on some of those mint leaves over there would freshen his breath.

***

While all this was going on, the mayor and the chairman of his party were both complacent, very complacent. They were satisfied that nothing untoward was happening.

***

But it was. Something very untoward was happening, very much so. And something even more untoward was about to happen. The mayor's daughter was getting herself all prettied up so she could go up on the mountainside to make it happen.

She wasn't going to take no for an answer today. She was willing to give the hermit some time to get used to the idea that they were going to play bouncy-bouncy, but she was going to wait only so long. If he wasn't ready by now, he was just going to have to deal with it as best he could.

The mayor's daughter checked out her hair, her makeup, her clothes. Check, check, check. Then she looked at everything again. Good, good, good. A dab of perfume.

All systems were go.

The mayor's daughter launched herself up onto the mountainside, on a trajectory leading to the hermit.

She reached his shack and knocked on the door. A weary-sounding voice from inside asked, "Who is it this time?"

As if he didn't know. "It's me," the mayor's daughter said. She pushed the door open and entered. He was sitting on his bed, reading. "Did you miss me?" she asked.

He put the book down. "I wish you wouldn't do this," he said.

"Oh, come on. What man would pass up the opportunity to play a little bouncy-bouncy with a firm, luscious, young lady such as I? What's not to like?"

"We've been through that," the hermit said.

"Don't you think I'm pretty?"

"I think you're very pretty. It's not a question of being pretty."

She sat on the bed next to him. "I wanted to make the effort to look extra nice for you. Doesn't that count for something?"

"I didn't ask you to make any effort."

"You're going to see a lot of effort tonight," she said.

That was that. There's no need to go on with the dialog. She wore him down just by sitting close to him, her hands doing certain things on him with just the right sort of touch, her soft, warm voice getting softer and warmer...

***

...and a shock wave ran through the village. A

subsonic rumble rippled through the ground, just below the surface. A deep, resonant voice, seemingly from nowhere, sang the "Ode to Joy," and it boomed out over the village with a tasteful amount of reverb. Thunderclouds gathered over the area and formed themselves into portraits of late nineteenth-century presidents. A stampede of aardvarks ran through the village. Don Quixote—his own bad self—came riding in on Rocinante, slowly and looking unsure of himself, as if lost. Ambrose Bierce disappeared again. Time reversed itself for precisely 7.8 minutes and then began flowing forward again...

***

...and after it was over, the hermit lay on his bed, naked, dehydrated, his vision blurred and his breathing weak. The mayor's daughter stayed with him until he recovered. She brought him water. She talked to him and rubbed him down.

He lay back and relaxed, and she walked around, checking out the shack. "What's this?" she asked.

"What's what?" He couldn't tell what she was looking at; his vision was still blurry.

She grabbed his coat and held it out at arm's length. "This thing is *hideous*!"

"Yeah, well, I never expected any fashion mavens for company."

***

When the mayor's daughter came home, her father was waiting for her. The telltale phenomena left no doubt as to what she had been doing.

"Where have you been?" he asked.

"Nowhere."

"What have you been doing?"

"Nothing."

"Who were you with?"

"No one."

"Well," he said, "that's a load off my mind. I thought you might have been playing bouncy-bouncy with that old hermit up on the mountainside."

"Oh, daddy, how could you think such a thing?"

"All this strange stuff was happening..."

"Daddy, I've seen that hermit. He's old and gruff, and he's all wrinkled up and dried out, and his hair and his beard are long and scraggly and gray, and his clothes don't fit, and he smells bad..."

"Smells bad? You got close enough to know how he smells?"

"You don't have to get close. Daddy, how could you think—how could you *think*—that I would want to play bouncy-bouncy with him?"

"Well, sweetheart..." the mayor was very uncertain of himself now. That is to say, he was more uncertain than usual. He wished he could be back at his office right at that moment, at work, where no one would expect anything of him.

"I went for a walk in the forest, just like always," she said. "That's *all* I did." With that, she went upstairs to her room, leaving daddy—her father—downstairs to gape at the place where she had been standing.

Well, he thought, if she was just out for a walk, maybe something else was causing all that stuff to happen.

Yeah, the only thing missing from *that* picture was

some sand for the mayor to bury his head in.

She had no sooner gotten to her room when her phone rang. It was her best friend. "You did it, didn't you?" the best friend said.

"Did what?"

"You went up there and seduced that hermit."

"What makes you think so?"

"Oh, come on. Everyone knows when you…well, when you do *that*."

"Oh, my gosh," the mayor's daughter said. "I didn't think all that stuff would spread out all the way back to the village."

"Well, it did. Everyone knows something happened somewhere."

"It happened, all right. It was pretty good, too. It was exciting to play bouncy-bouncy with someone like him. I know it sounds funny, but he had, uh…a certain kind of wisdom that made it better."

"Wisdom."

"Yeah. And I think he liked it, too. He was very enthusiastic about it, once we got started."

"Would he have liked it if he had known they're threatening guys who play with you? If he knew about that one guy who disappeared altogether?"

"What's going to happen? No one knows who he is. Most people don't even think he actually exists. The people who do, don't think I would want to get near him."

"I hope it stays that way."

***

The chairman was on the phone, shouting incoherently.

He was upset. He was calling his friendly police officers and telling them to meet him at the secret abandoned warehouse. "Now," he said. "I need you there *right now*." It didn't matter that they were in the middle of dinner, or making love to their wives, or helping their children with their homework. It didn't even matter if they were watching *Ninja Warrior* reruns. This was a political crisis.

At the warehouse, the chairman paced back and forth in front of the officers. They had ordered pizza to be delivered. Some of the guys were munching on sausage and onion, and those who were slightly more adventurous were having the combo lemon-tofu-pickle relish pizza.

"We have to stop this," the chairman said. "By itself, the girl's behavior is a political embarrassment for the party. But now that we've seen she's continuing after all we've done to stop her, the embarrassment is much, much greater."

The guys looked at him with big, blank eyes.

He continued. "I want her under twenty-four-hour surveillance. The next time she's playing bouncy-bouncy, I want someone right there who knows where she is and who she's with. I want the guy nabbed and brought here immediately. I. Want. This. Stopped. Now. Any questions?"

"Do you want this last slice of pizza?" one of the guys asked. "Because if you don't..."

"Take it," the chairman said. He rolled his eyes. That is to say, he moved them around in their sockets. He didn't take them out and roll them across the floor.

***

The hermit stayed in bed to finish recovering. He dreamed his shack burned down. He dreamed that he was on the Bridge of Constant Focus, and the drawbridge part flopped over backward and crushed him as he sat next to it. He dreamed that Alvin Loner was filing unfavorable reports about him to hermit school, reports full of words like "incompetent" and "embarrassment to the hermit community." He dreamed that his carrot wine had gone bad. He dreamed that the dancing goldfish morphed into large, half-fish-half-person creatures who grabbed him and dropped him into a huge fish bowl.

Gradually the dreams subsided, and the hermit drifted into a deeper, dreamless sleep.

He woke up feeling that he had some sort of otherworldly hangover. He also felt in love, but he thought it was probably a temporary thing. He hoped so, anyway.

And then he thought that he had reached a dreadful state of affairs. His spiritual journey was over and done with—he was sure of it—over and done with, aborted just a few steps away from his goal. He had suddenly failed after so many, many years of progress. And all because of one girl who wanted him to…to do what he had done.

The hermit burrowed in under his blanket and went back to sleep.

***

But he wasn't allowed to sleep for very long. Once again, he heard a knock, and before he could say anything, the door swung open, and the mysterious stranger stepped in. “Hello, hermit,” he said.

“My gosh,” the hermit moaned. “Can’t you people leave me alone?”

“We could, but then we wouldn’t have a story. Why do you want to be alone, anyway?”

“Well, it’s, like, my job description. Duh.”

The mysterious stranger sat on the edge of the bed. “How did you like your little encounter with the mayor’s daughter?”

“It wasn’t little, believe me.”

“You enjoyed it, didn’t you?”

“That’s not the problem.”

“You’re not feeling guilty about it, are you?”

“Guilty isn’t the word. I just think it was a bad career move.”

“Maybe it’s time for a career change,” the mysterious stranger said.

“I don’t want a career change. I’ve been happy as a hermit all along. If I *did* want a career change, I would be too old for it now, anyway.”

“That’s a rather defeatist attitude.”

“It’s true,” the hermit said. “Now, if you had some reason for walking in on me, tell me what’s on your mind. I’m not inclined to sit here and listen to you prattle on about nothing.”

“I just wanted to tell you,” the mysterious stranger said, leaning in close and adopting a buddy-buddy attitude, “that the mayor’s daughter really, really, really thought you were a great lover.”

“Pish-posh.”

“No, really. You have a certain wisdom in your style that none of the other guys have.”

"Wisdom in my style?"

"Something like that. Wisdom. She likes wisdom."

"That's too bad," the hermit said. "The wisdom is gone."

"How could it be gone?"

"Not that it's any of your business, but my spiritual journey has gotten all messed up. I try to meditate, and everything goes wrong. To be honest, I think it may have something to do with her."

"I'm sorry to hear that. But I don't think it's fair to blame your problems on other people."

"I don't think she deliberately set out to mess me up. It just happened to work out that way. I mean, that's the way I would see it if I wanted to talk about it, which I don't."

The mysterious stranger nodded. "You know," he said, "I'm willing to bet..." he stopped and leaned forward. "All that stuff about sex and the mayor's daughter, and all that, I'm willing to bet that it's a problem only because you think it has to be a problem. I think that if you could relax and enjoy it for what it is, you would have no problem of any type. None whatsoever."

"No, you got it all wrong," the hermit said. "They taught us at hermit school that we had to give up women. No sex. They were very emphatic about it."

"Of course they were. That school is a great, big, fat, hairy scam. They charge preposterous amounts of money for the appearance of teaching people things that, in reality, don't need to be taught. They tell all these strong, healthy young men they have to give up women, and that helps make the whole thing seem authentic."

"I don't want to talk about it."

"I think you have, maybe, a little bit of a clue," the mysterious stranger went on. "You got cleaned up for her."

"It was a moment of weakness, and I still don't want to talk about it."

The mysterious stranger stood up. "You don't have to. All I wanted was to tell you things look good in regard to the mayor's daughter."

***

Let's just say that if the hermit could relax and quit thinking of sex as a problem, which he couldn't, then yes indeed, things would have been looking good. The mayor's daughter was already looking forward to their next date, planning what she would wear, and so on.

He wasn't looking forward to anything. He was hoping that the mysterious stranger had lied to him, that she had been disappointed and would go off looking for someone else and leave him alone. Since he was in a deep blue funk over his meditation problems, problems that she had exacerbated—or maybe even caused—he wasn't in the mood to have her over for so much as a game of rock, paper, scissors.

He might have a tiny, little chance of solving his meditation problems, but only if he could be rid of the girl. Even if he didn't solve anything, he still didn't want her around. He was going to live the rest of his life as a hermit. If it meant being a hermit who hadn't attained his goal, it would be unfortunate, but so be it.

And yet he remembered how it was, the smoothness of her skin, the softness of her touch, the warmth of her...of her everything. He knew that throughout history, men had repeatedly—and very often cheerfully—done very stupid things because of women. Most men had. He would be in good company.

CHAPTER TWELVE

The police officers friendly with the chairman were extra careful to watch for the mayor's daughter to go up on the mountainside. They were pretty sure that was where she had been the last time the phenomena hit.

Sure enough, a few days later, one of them spotted her walking along the road leading out of the village. The officer watched as she went out into the countryside and took a sharp left to go off the road and head up onto the mountain.

He called the chairman, and a flurry of other calls ensued. Other officers were secretly dispatched. Party officials were notified.

The officer followed at a discreet distance. He thought she seemed to be very purposeful, as if she were going somewhere for an important reason. No, this didn't look like a casual stroll through the woods just for the sake of enjoying the bountiful wonders of nature.

She led the officer through the forest and higher up onto the mountain. Eventually she came to a shack in the middle of a clearing. He hid behind a tree and watched as she tapped, oh so politely, on the door. Without waiting for an answer, she stepped inside.

The officer called the chairman again. "I think she's visiting that hermit," he whispered. "She went into a homemade shack on the mountainside."

"Oh, this is great," the chairman said. "We're finally going to bust this wide open."

The officer gave the chairman directions to the shack. "Stay put," the chairman said. "I'm going to send a couple more guys. I'll get 'em up there ASAP. In the meantime, just keep watching. Call back if anything happens."

"Yes, sir."

"And don't go in until the weird stuff starts happening. We want to catch them in the act."

"Yes, sir."

***

In the shack, the mayor's daughter was sitting next to the hermit on his bed. "I've been thinking about you," she said.

"You don't have to do that on my account."

"I'm doing it on *my* account. You were a very good lover, I'll have you know." She placed her hand on his knee and squeezed gently, as if considering a cantaloupe in the produce section.

"Yeah, whatever." He moved her hand away.

"Didn't you like it? It seemed to me you were really getting into it."

"A few moments of pleasure isn't worth losing a lifetime of spiritual attainment."

"Wow, I bet you're really the life of the party."

"I don't go to parties."

"It wouldn't hurt you to go to a party occasionally.

Have a little bit of fun. I think you're too serious minded."

"I'm too old to change now."

They bantered a bit more, verging on escalating into an argument but never quite getting there.

And outside, other officers were showing up. "They're in that shack," the first one said.

"Are we ready to go in?"

"No, we have to wait until the weird stuff starts. We want to catch them in the act."

They made sure their guns were loaded and watched the shack with great intensity. They watched it with so much intensity that the hermit and the mayor's daughter, inside, could feel it. They didn't know what the feeling was, though. The hermit thought it was the feeling of the universe trying to crush him. The mayor's daughter thought it might be gas from the burrito she had had for lunch.

And the police officers thought the lovebirds were taking an awfully long time to get started. "What are they doing in there?" one of them wondered.

"Maybe they're going through the 'How was your day, honey?' routine."

"The dude's a hermit. What's going to happen to him that's worth talking about?"

"Maybe the girl's doing all the talking. She probably has plenty to talk about."

"What's she going to say that he would want to hear?"

"Well, then, maybe they're playing Chinese checkers."

"Not likely. They have better games to play."

"They're not playing them, are they?"

"They will, my friend. They will."

So the officers waited outside. They sat waiting for the Big Disturbance, the wave of unnatural phenomena that would mean the mayor's daughter was up to her antics again, playing bouncy-bouncy with the hermit. When it started, they could proceed with their raid. They could throw a bucket of ice water on the amorous couple. They would just throw a blanket over the mayor's daughter because they couldn't treat her very harshly...but the hermit, ah, the hermit. They could drag him out by his feet, all naked and stuff (the hermit being the naked one, that is, not the officers), and he would probably be trying to cover his private areas with his hands, and his eyes would be big and round and wide open and shiny like spinner hubcaps on a car coming out of a carwash. Then they could rough him up a little and maybe ridicule him.

Yeah, the officers were looking forward to their little raid. Interrupting a couple of people in the middle of playing bouncy-bouncy was about as exciting as law enforcement got in the village. (Years later there would be a crime wave, with a war between two competing gangs selling counterfeit designer shoelaces, but that was to be many, many years later.)

And inside, the hermit and the mayor's daughter were still talking.

"Even if I wanted to play bouncy-bouncy, I wouldn't be in the mood for it right now," he said. "I'm feeling down because my spiritual journey crashed and burned."

"How does a journey crash?"

The hermit gave her a withering look. "Don't expect me to be sharp with my metaphors at a time like this."

"I think a little physical activity is just what you need." Her hand went back to his knee.

"I think it's the last thing I need."

"What's it going to hurt?" Her hand went higher up his thigh. He let it stay there.

"It would probably hurt my chances of being able to get my meditative technique back in order."

It was becoming clear to the mayor's daughter that she wasn't going to get anywhere this time. He was just too depressed. She stood up. "All right, I'll go if you want me to."

"I want you to."

She gave him a little peck on the cheek. "I'm not giving up, though. I think you and I can do some monumental stuff together."

"Yeah, monumental. Whatever."

Outside, the officers saw the mayor's daughter come out of the shack. What was this all about? Was she going out for beer, or what? They clearly hadn't been misbehaving; there had been no phenomena, and besides, her clothing and hair looked remarkably un-disheveled. It was almost as if she had just that instant gotten finished fixing herself up to look pretty.

The officers looked at one another in puzzled puzzlement as the mayor's daughter walked on down to the foot of the mountain, into the village, and back home.

When the chairman found out, he knew that only one explanation was possible: the mayor's daughter had known she was being followed. She and the hermit were onto them.

***

It was festival time in the village. The festival wasn't a tradition because the village hadn't been operating long enough to have anything you could call a tradition, but some of the people were hoping it might become one. Everyone needs traditions, they thought.

And so it was that some of the village movers and shakers organized this festival, which was called the Village's Annual Celebration Under Opulent, Ubiquitous Stars. Music was going to play. People were going to dress up in costumes and dance in the streets. They were going to eat fried food and drink wine and play games. And not just computer games, either. Real-life games such as ice hockey and polo and underwater ping-pong. There would be a unicorn show. It was going to be something like Mardi Gras, except more village-like.

Plans had been underway for months. Musicians had rehearsed, and athletes had practiced. Chefs had created elaborate new recipes. Businesses had created special advertising and worked on clever product placement ideas. Everyone was very enthusiastic, in the spirit of the occasion. Carnival rides were set up in a public park near the middle of the village.

As the festival came closer, banners were put up along the streets. Crews were sent out to put an extra coat of wax on the sidewalks. No detail, no matter how small, was overlooked: extra toilet seat covers were put in the public rest-rooms.

The mayor's daughter and her best friend had been working on their costumes. The best friend was going to be some sort of mutant combination of a honeybee, an owl, a minor demon, a killer robot from the sixteenth dimension, and Thomas Jefferson. The mayor's daughter was going to be a bunny rabbit.

The festival was going to start on a Friday, in the early afternoon, and last until late Sunday night. (Yes, people were going to be late to work the next day. It was okay, though, because their bosses were also going to be late.) Streets were blocked off. Businesses were closed and locked up. Television crews set up cameras in strategic locations, although it wasn't clear why they would do that because everyone was going to be at the festival rather than home watching TV.

Friday was a clear day, sunny and warm, with only a single cloud (shaped like Woody Allen) in the sky.

Things kicked off with a big parade down Main Street. The grand marshal was the first—and so far only—celebrity the village had produced. He was Arnie MacAroon, and he had won the National Philo T. Farnsworth Lookalike Contest two years previously. He took second place the following year. Despite his rise to success, Arnie had tired of life in the big city and returned to the village to live a life of ordinary ordinariness. People were impressed by how down to earth he was.

As grand marshal, Arnie rode in a convertible and waved to the crowd. His wife sat next to him and waved, too. She had a very pretty smile.

The mayor rode in the follow-up car. He tried to look bright and friendly, but inwardly he was on edge because everyone was paying attention to Arnie. It wasn't fair, the mayor thought. He needed the voters' attention. But the harsh fact is that you can't compete with a celebrity. Maybe he could ask Arnie for an endorsement in the next election. Yeah, that would be a pretty compelling vote getter.

A marching band followed the mayor, playing a song the official village composer had written for the occasion, "Our Village Is a Pretty Spiffy Place." The arrangement was full of brass and bass drums and cymbals—very rousing and spirited, designed to instill a feeling of civic pride among the people. The mayor made a mental note to himself to propose that the song be declared the official village song.

Parade floats were next. First was a float of the village mascot, a hamster with a prosthetic leg. Yes, there's a story that explains how a hamster with a prosthetic leg came to be the village mascot, but we don't need to get into it here. Suffice to say that a thirty-foot-long float of a hamster with a prosthetic leg looked quite spectacular. Children pointed at it in awe, and adults stood around whispering to one another.

The next float was a large representation of the mayor, simply because the parade organizers couldn't think of any other ideas for a float. They got his eyes the wrong color, but otherwise it looked just like him. Well, reasonably like him. The village's best artist wasn't available because she had gone to New York City for a medical procedure. That was the story, anyway. The real reason was simply that she had called a cab to go to an appointment with someone who wanted to commission a work of art, the driver got lost, and she ended up in New York City. That's how it goes sometimes.

But I digress. After the floats came the unicorns that were going to be in the unicorn show. They marched down the street in a precise formation meant to look like a slice of French toast, the official village food, but which really looked more like Humphrey Bogart's left ear. After the parade was over, they would be taken to the Arnie MacAroon Village Arena.

And finally, all the little kindergarten children followed up in the rear, laughing and singing and wearing T-shirts that had a picture of a hamster with a prosthetic leg screen printed on them.

Everyone lined the streets, in high spirits as the parade passed.

The mayor's daughter rode on the float of her father. His float-figure was posed seated on a chair, and she sat on his lap waving to the crowd. Her teeth were white and her hair was brushed attractively, and she wore a pink dress with green and purple flowers on it, a festive dress for a festive occasion.

And as she rode through the streets, she eyeballed all the young fellas in the crowd. She could see all of them because, as we've already seen, everyone in the village was there to watch the parade. She could see the guys she had already played with, and guys she wanted to play with but hadn't, and guys she didn't particularly care about playing with.

The guys were eyeballing her, too. Guys she had already played with were nursing a little bit of love for her, and they wished they could play with her some more. Guys she hadn't played with—that is to say, the single guys who were inclined to do such things—those guys felt a little sad because now, with the dire threat of disappearing if they so much as shook her hand, they knew they would never be able to play a legendary game of bouncy-bouncy with the mayor's daughter. In fact, several of them had started writing lengthy, introspective novels about missed opportunities.

Police officers posted along the parade route eyeballed the mayor's daughter and the single guys in the crowd. They, the officers, had to make sure that nothing untoward was going on.

What could happen in the middle of a parade? Well, they didn't know. They suspected—that is to say, the party chairman suspected—that if the mayor's daughter could be sneaky enough to do something, the unnatural phenomena could very well pass unnoticed in the middle of the festival, what with all the exotic activity. If the mayor's daughter had the same suspicion, she might just decide to take advantage of it. For example, she might drag some poor sap inside the float of the hamster with the prosthetic leg, which was hollow, and...oh, boy! That was why they had to be especially vigilant.

The party chairman walked alongside the parade, watching the mayor's daughter. Even though he had his friendly police officers watching her, he really wasn't comfortable with leaving the job to someone else. He saw how she was checking out the guys, the look on her face.

But he needn't have worried. She didn't have any crazy schemes up her sleeve—or anywhere else, for that matter. She was just enjoying the festival.

So the parade went down Main Street, all the way to the edge of town. As it ended, the people cheered and swarmed into the streets. A rock band started playing. They were called The Mischievous Elves and they didn't know how to play any songs all the way through, so somehow their set ended up being a medley of the first halves of a bunch of songs. The sad fact was that the amount of musical talent in the village was surprisingly limited.

The festival went on.

Up on the mountainside, the hermit could hear the noise. He walked out to an area overlooking the village, where he could get a clear view of what was happening.

It was madness. From such a distance he couldn't make out much, but he could see the crowds swirling about in the streets and the band playing onstage and the carnival rides operating in the park.

He watched, fascinated. He hadn't seen so many people or so much activity...ever.

The mayor's daughter reached the end of the parade route and climbed off of her float, with a couple of strong young men helping her step down. They were just a little bit nervous to have even this much contact with her, but of course the chairman understood they were merely being gallant. The mayor's daughter, seeing that she was under the watchful eye of the chairman, decided to play a little prank on him. That mischievous girl.

She walked up to one of the strong young men and whispered in his ear. She told him that his friend had asked her to ask him to meet the friend behind the library in ten minutes. She watched as the strong young man walked off toward the library. Out of the corner of her eye, she saw the chairman watching. His mouth dropped open, looking like something you'd see in a nature film. He took a cell phone out of his pocket. Nervous and fumbling, he managed with some difficulty to make a call. Very good, very good so far, the mayor's daughter thought.

Then she walked up to another strong young man and told him the same thing. Once again, the chairman made another phone call.

Smiling inwardly—well, and outwardly, too—the

mayor's daughter went to an outdoor cafe and sat down. She ordered a glass of red wine and the cafe's specialty: a tray of diced camel humps, deep fried in pancake batter spiced with a single tear from a six-week-old kitten, each piece served on the lower half of a hummingbird's beak. It was what they called a delicacy.

She sat there enjoying her lunch while the crowd milled around. People were laughing and singing and shouting and playing hopscotch. It didn't escape the mayor's daughter's notice that she didn't see any police officers patrolling around.

After a while her best friend happened to come along. She saw the mayor's daughter and sat down with her.

"Have some fried camel humps," the mayor's daughter said.

"I just love this festival," the best friend said, popping a fried camel hump cube into her mouth.

The mayor's daughter leaned over the table, close to her best friend so she could speak low. "I played a joke on my daddy's party chairman."

"What did you do?"

The mayor's daughter told her best friend about sending the guys off to meet each other behind the library. "The chairman got excited and started making phone calls," she said. "I'm pretty sure he had his friendly police officers follow them."

"What good does that do?"

"It's just for fun."

"He's going to be mad at you."

"What did I do? I just whispered in a couple guys' ears. Why would he have a problem with that?"

A couple of blocks away, several officers were staked

out just around the corner from the meeting place where the mayor's daughter had sent those two guys. The guys were standing there in the alley looking confused. They didn't know each other; the mayor's daughter had just picked a couple of guys at random.

The officers waited for the mayor's daughter, who wasn't going to show up.

The guys waited for friends who weren't going to show up.

And when the mayor's daughter and her best friend finished at the cafe, they paid and went to check out the rides in the public park.

***

That night the chairman thought about what he was going to do next. It seemed clear that the mayor's daughter was onto him. She knew he was keeping tabs on her, and she was taking countermeasures. She was sending his people off on wild goose chases.

But he had an idea. He could have hidden cameras set up along the path to the hermit's shack. That way, he wouldn't have to have guys follow her. He wouldn't have to have guys patrol the outskirts of the village watching for her to go up there. To all appearances—that is to say, as far as the mayor's daughter could see—it would look as though he had given up trying to watch her. The cameras, discreetly placed, would tell him when she was on her way to visit the hermit. Then he could send his guys up the mountainside. They would get there in time to catch the lovebirds in the middle of doing whatever they might be doing.

Yes, he was quite pleased with himself for thinking

of such a devious plan. The girl was a worthy opponent, but he was just a little bit worthier, yes indeed.

The chairman went to his computer and searched for hidden cameras on the Internet. He was surprised to find a whole lot of porn sites from that particular search, but eventually he was able to find what he needed. He would arrange to have the cameras set up Monday during the day, when the mayor's daughter was at work. That way, there would be no chance that she'd suddenly decide to go up on the mountain at a time when she might catch the installers at work.

Everything was coming together quite well, he thought.

***

Up on the mountain, the hermit was still watching the festival. It was spectacular at night, from a distance. The lights were bright and colorful, and the noise was even louder. Maybe sound carried better at night. He didn't know. He just thought it was nice to watch, even if he would never consider, not in thirteen million years, going down there and getting into it himself.

It reminded him of a carnival his parents had taken him to when he was seven. They had walked through the midway, the little hermit-to-be in the middle, holding a parent's hand with each of his, activity swirling about them like a choreographed, mechanical madness. The hermit remembered thinking he would have been scared had he been by himself, but he felt safe and very secure between his parents.

He hadn't seen them in fifty years.

The hermit became sleepy. He wasn't given to

sleeping outside, but he kind of felt he wanted to this time. He lay down on the soft grass and relaxed, and with the sounds of the festival in the background, he quickly slipped into a deep sleep.

He didn't dream.

***

At the festival, the unicorn show took place the next day. A panel of expert judges had flown in from such places as Las Vegas, Dallas, and Atlanta. The unicorn owners, very proud and very nervous, had trained their pets to perform dance and acrobatic routines with the grace and precision of a fancy New York PR firm covering up someone's political scandal. The judges were going to grade them on appearance, obedience, and the performance of two dance routines—one required routine that all of them would do, and one free routine in which they could do anything the owners could train them to do. Many of the routines were beautiful enough to bring tears to the spectators' eyes, as the unicorn is a very graceful and intelligent creature. They also have a sort of low-level telepathy that allows them to make people think their dance routines are better than they really are.

The mayor's daughter and her best friend went to the unicorn show. They had never had any particular interest in unicorns before, but caught up in the spirit of the festival, they decided it might be fun. In fact, as they sat in the Arnie MacAroon Village Arena waiting for the proceedings to proceed, they were getting—shall I say it?—excited.

The show opened with the owners leading the

unicorns onto the main floor in a well-coordinated procession. When they were all inside, they lined up in three rows, standing at attention. The judges made the rounds, examining each animal, considering grooming, the sheen of the fur, the sparkle of the eyes, the sweetness of breath (a unicorn's breath should smell like honey). Each owner would give her unicorn a few commands such as sit, lie down, and whatnot.

Then the dance routines commenced. Each unicorn took the stage, a large platform in the middle of the arena floor, and did its required dance routine. The judges scored the dance. After that, they did the free routines. One did the Charleston to a Marilyn Manson song.

The mayor's daughter and her best friend watched, rapt.

After the dance routines, the Mischievous Elves took the stage and played a couple of rockin' little numbers while the judges tabulated their results.

The winner was a blue unicorn named Fritz. The audience erupted in excitement; Fritz had been a favorite, and everyone was glad he won. His owner was crying for joy as the head judge awarded her a wreath and a big, ceremonial check for a thousand dollars.

"I wish I had a unicorn," the mayor's daughter said.

***

No special events were planned for the third day. Most of the budget for the festival had gone into stuff that had taken place the first two days. So people just wandered around on the streets, in costume, drinking and stumbling around.

Up on the hillside, the hermit sensed a change in the atmosphere in the village. It's not that it was a sinister change, not by any means. The feeling just wasn't up to the high standards set during the first two days.

The people in the village felt it as well. They tried to whip up more enthusiasm, but it just wasn't there. Well, maybe next year's festival would be able to sustain the mood better.

***

Monday morning the mayor's daughter went to work, and the installers went up onto the mountainside to set up the hidden cameras. They weren't sure what was going on; why on earth would anyone feel the need to place hidden cameras in a forest? Well, no matter. They were getting paid, and that was all they cared about.

They had to climb the trees, up high, and fix up the cameras so they were peeking through the leaves. The cameras themselves were in camouflage-painted housings. It wasn't likely that anyone would notice them.

The installers set up a dozen cameras along a trail leading from the foot of the mountain up to a clearing where a rough-looking shack stood. "I wonder if anyone lives there," one of the installers said.

"I doubt it," another one said. "It doesn't look like it's fit to use as a tool shed, let alone as a place to live."

"Maybe it's some type of top-secret government facility. Like, maybe you go in there, and there's an elevator that goes down to a huge underground complex where they're conducting nuclear research and brainwashing political prisoners and doing autopsies on aliens and stuff."

"You've been watching too many movies."

"Maybe so, but it seems obvious that they want these cameras here to watch for people coming to the shack."

The other installer thought it over for a moment. "Makes sense," he said. "Maybe we'd better not talk about it. Sometimes people end up disappearing when they get too curious about top-secret government facilities."

The installers finished their work in silence.

***

By the end of the day, the chairman had a video monitor on his desk with a feed from the hidden cameras. He was so pleased about it that he spent the whole night looking at pictures from the mountainside, switching from one camera to another. The pictures didn't show anything but dim outlines in the dark, but it didn't matter. If her past behavior was any indication, the mayor's daughter would be going up there in the daytime.

***

That is to say, she would be going in the daytime if she was going. The mayor's daughter was unsure. She wanted to go back and take another shot at trying to get the hermit to play bouncy-bouncy, but he had seemed so...blue the last time she had been there. His meditation problems really had him down.

Maybe she shouldn't bother him. He was, after all, a man of wisdom. Maybe she should just accept the idea that he knew what was best for himself.

She thought about all this through her day at work, and through her dinnertime shift at the soup kitchen, and in the evening after she went home.

CHAPTER THIRTEEN

And as the hermit slept, he had another dream. He dreamed he was in The Golden Wolf and the Beginning of Destiny, in the tunnel, and he came to the statue of the wolf.

As the hermit got closer, he could see that the wolf wasn't a statue. It was a real wolf, flesh and blood, and he was wearing a flea collar. His fur was a golden blond color. It didn't glow, but it had a nice sheen. The hermit wondered what brand of shampoo he used. Or maybe it a conditioner that gave it that look. He, the wolf, lay there on the floor of the tunnel, a sort of neutral expression on his face. Maybe he had just awakened from a nap.

The wolf rose to his feet. The hermit could see that the key to the exit was on the floor, where the wolf had been lying. The wolf stepped back so the key was in front of him, and he nudged it forward with his nose. He looked up at the hermit expectantly.

The hermit didn't know what to do. He looked at the wolf, then at the key, then at the wolf. He was just a little afraid of the wolf. He wasn't sure what it would do, but he knew it could mess him up pretty bad if it decided to attack.

The wolf sighed impatiently and nudged the key forward again.

The hermit continued standing there, puzzled.

The wolf finally spoke. "Listen, clown," it said, "I'm not supposed to be able to speak, but it seems clear that you're not going to get the message unless I spell it out for you—as if pushing the key toward you isn't obvious enough. You're supposed to take the key. Bend down and pick it up. Continue through the tunnel. I'm not going to hurt you. I'm trying to help you, you goofball."

The hermit continued standing there, puzzled.

"Take the daggone key!"

At that point the hermit woke up. He sat up in bed a few moments and then went outside. It was dark, dark.

He stood out there, being part of the night, wondering what to do. He thought the dream was telling him to try his meditation again, that it would be okay now. But he wasn't sure. He didn't trust his instincts. All these recent events had been too weird, too intense for him to just shrug it off now and go about his business.

Further, it was tied in with that girl, and she... well, she had seemed singlemindedly intent upon getting him to play bouncy-bouncy. He wasn't sure that he hadn't somehow messed himself up permanently by playing with her the one time. In any case, she was going to come back, no doubt about it. She had taken no for an answer that last time, but he knew that wasn't going to be the end of the story.

What would Alvin Loner do?

He probably wouldn't get into a situation like this.

The hermit went for a little walk, fifteen minutes up toward the top of the mountain and then back down to his shack. Arriving home, he was invigorated. Walking made him feel strong. He lingered outside for a while longer and then went inside to meditate.

He sat on his bed and assumed his meditative position. It felt strange. He hadn't meditated for several days; until now he had never gone longer than a single day without meditating. Now it was awkward, a "once familiar thing turned unfamiliar" situation, sort of like the way you might feel if you're out at the mall and happen to come face to face with an ex-girlfriend or boyfriend and you don't quite know what to say.

Perhaps he needed to try the pre-meditative state first to get ready. He took the pose and quickly found himself in the white room. It was a bit chillier than it had been before, but otherwise nothing seemed amiss. He wasn't even sure that the chill was amiss, really.

The hermit stayed there for some short of length of time. He didn't know how long. He didn't care, and it didn't matter. He decided it was time to come back out when he heard a very faint Claptonesque guitar tune from off in the distance—maybe from the twenty-third dimension.

And then into The Golden Wolf and the Beginning of Destiny. He was once again at the entrance to the tunnel. He entered and followed the tunnel through its winding curves, feeling his way carefully through the darkness.

At last he came to the wolf statue. He hadn't realized it until just now, but he had been afraid, just ever so slightly afraid, that the wolf would be alive as it had been in the dream.

It was a statue, though. It stood there in its mid-run pose, giving the feel of being dynamic.

The hermit reached into the wolf's mouth and felt around for the key.

He pulled out a cupcake. A green cupcake.

He sat on the ground and regarded the wolf sadly. This was the last straw, the *last freakin' straw.*

***

The next evening, the mayor's daughter was hanging out in her room with her best friend, playing CDs and talking about stuff.

"That cute guy who works at the bicycle shop asked me out," the best friend said.

"What did you tell him?"

"I told him yes. He's cute. He has a nice smile, and he's funny. He told me a joke: A skeleton walked into a bar and said, 'Give me a beer and a mop.'"

"A guy who can tell jokes like that, you want to keep him. But can he play bouncy-bouncy?"

"I don't know," the best friend said. "I'm not thinking about that, anyway. We're only going out to see a movie."

"Yeah, but at some point you're going to need to know."

"I'll worry about that when the time comes. If it comes."

"See, best friend, that's where we're different. I don't want to wait that long, and just say I'll worry about it when the time comes, and not have any idea when the time is going to come. I need my bouncy-bouncy."

"I need it, too," the best friend said. "Don't get me wrong, I need my bouncy-bouncy. Everybody does. It's just that I like it better if I know I have something in common with the guy besides just, like, each of us thinking the other is hot."

The mayor's daughter thought about it for a moment. "Well, what happens when you go out with a guy for a while, and then you decide to play with him, and it turns out he's not very good at it? Then you've wasted all that time going out with him. It's better to find out early so you can move on."

"No, it's not like that. If I know the guy and like him, I can work with him."

And that gave the mayor's daughter something to think about. If the hermit was reluctant, maybe it was just because he didn't see that the two of them had much in common. Being the spiritual man of spiritualism that he was, it made sense that he would feel that way. If she spent a little time trying to get to know him better, and letting him get to know her better, he might be more relaxed about it. And she knew that they had one important thing in common: she had become interested in hermitism. That, if nothing else, would give them something else to talk about for a while.

Yeah, she would take one more shot at it. She would go up on that mountainside, talk to the hermit, and take one more shot at it.

***

The following Saturday, the mayor's daughter got ready to go visit the hermit. She didn't fix herself up all gorgeous the way she had done before. She wanted to look nice, but just a sort of everyday kind of nice, fitting her mood. She put on her best Duran Duran T-shirt and orange corduroy pants.

And up the mountainside she went, the mayor's daughter, up the mountainside to see the hermit. As she walked, she rehearsed in her head the things she would talk to him about. She would tell him about going to school and going to work. She would tell him the story of the time she went to New York City and had dinner in a fancy restaurant. She would tell him about the time, just about a year ago, when she was in the tavern trolling for a guy, and a fella came up to her and said he was going to leave home and become a hermit the next day, and he would like to remember his last night in society as having been a warm, intimate one with a lovely lady such as her.

No, better not tell him about that last story. He might not want to hear about other guys she had played with. That kind of thing bothered some guys.

***

As the mayor's daughter made her trip up the mountainside, the chairman sat in his office watching on his video monitor. He smiled and nodded. Yes, this was it. This was going to be the final scene in this whole sorry drama, and soon they would be able to put it all behind them and move on.

Yes.

He picked up the phone and started calling his friendly officers. Some of them were on duty, but three were available to go chase after the hermit up there on the mountainside. That would be plenty. How many guys do you need to handle a seventy-something-year-old hermit, anyway? Not very many, he was willing to bet.

The orders were the same: the officers were supposed to go up the mountainside, to the clearing where the hermit's shack was, hide behind a tree, and wait for the weird stuff to start. Then they would move in and catch 'em in the act—or maybe we should say catcheminthеact, all one word, because it would be just that sudden. Yeah, she might have known she was being followed that one time, but this time...this time, she wasn't actually being followed, so there was nothing to know. She wouldn't suspect a thing.

The chairman sat back and chuckled. An image of the hermit's shack flickered on his video monitor. He hoped—the chairman, that is—that the hidden cameras would survive the weird phenomena. During a couple of previous episodes, television broadcasting had been disrupted. The chairman hoped nothing like that would happen today. He wanted to see the hermit getting dragged out of that shack.

Now, let it be said that the chairman wasn't a cruel man, and he had nothing against the hermit. Under other circumstances—under any other circumstances—he would have been happy to leave the hermit up there all by himself, doing whatever he was doing. (What the heck did hermits do, anyway? he wondered. He would have to ask the hermit when he had the opportunity.) The chairman was, however, ruthless, and he had his own priorities. The unfortunate fact, the bottom line, was that this hermit guy had unknowingly gotten himself involved in something the chairman couldn't allow.

So although the chairman wasn't going to enjoy

seeing misfortune befall that poor sap up there on the mountainside, he was going to relish very much seeing his sticky little problem being solved.

***

In the hermit's shack, the mayor's daughter was talking to the hermit, person to person. "How do you put thoughts about women out of your mind?" she asked.

Like everyone (or almost everyone), the hermit was flattered that she wanted to talk about him and the things he was interested in. He got the impression that she wasn't just making idle chit-chat until she could lead up to something else. She really wanted to know. "It's not easy at first," he said. "When you're a young fella, strong and healthy with all kinds of hormones surging through your body, it's very difficult. It requires a special discipline. They teach you about it in hermit school."

"They have a whole course to teach you how not to think about women?"

"Oh, not just one course. It has three levels: beginning, intermediate, and advanced. If you don't do well in those courses, you're in for a very miserable life as a hermit."

"I can imagine. What do they teach you?"

"At first, they start out teaching you how to think of other things to distract yourself. It's a sort of mental discipline. In the advanced course, they teach body control techniques. They teach you how to lower your testosterone using your mind to control it. It's very difficult."

"I bet it is."

"Yes," the hermit said. And then—here's where he made his fatal mistake, but he had become so comfortable and trusting with this girl that he let his guard down—he added, "I was never very good at it."

(At this point, or maybe even earlier in the story, the attentive reader may be wondering how our hermit was one of the best students at the hermit school when there were so many things he wasn't very good at. Well, the thing is, the other students were even worse.)

And the mayor's daughter immediately thought this meant she could—*should*—plunge forward, full speed ahead. "So," she purred, putting her hand on his thigh, "if I were to do this, our 'friend' down there might, uh, take notice?"

The hermit, as expected, moved her hand away. "He would. But unlike you, I see that as a problem."

"Why? Everybody needs to play bouncy-bouncy occasionally. It's just the way we're wired."

"The way we're wired?"

"Sure. You have to breathe and eat. You have to get your exercise, and you have to rest. And you have to play bouncy-bouncy."

"How many times to I have to explain? Playing bouncy-bouncy is sort of the opposite of being a hermit."

"I don't know," the mayor's daughter said. "Maybe it's not."

"Look, you seem like a nice girl. But with all due respect, you're not the one who went to hermit school. I know what being a hermit is all about."

"I know you went to hermit school. I'm just saying, maybe it's possible that they're wrong about playing bouncy-bouncy. Maybe you can, like, indulge yourself a little bit, from time to time, and still be a good hermit."

"I don't see how."

Outside, the officers were waiting. They were getting impatient, looking at one another questioningly, shrugging their shoulders, shaking their heads in puzzlement. This was taking a long time, but they had to wait.

And so did the chairman.

"I've done a lot of reading about being a hermit," the mayor's daughter said, inside the shack. "I don't think you have to give up your bouncy-bouncy. It's not as if I want to come here and live with you."

The hermit continued to protest. What you should understand, though, is that he was just going through the motions. Saying no was just an automatic response; it had been programmed into his brain the same way it's programmed into young children to crave sugary breakfast cereals. But he was so worn out and discouraged from his meditation problems that he didn't have the energy or the will to mount a truly determined resistance.

And he did feel comfortable with the girl. That is to say, he felt comfortable with her in just about every way except for her...uh...personal overtures. And if the overtures didn't have to be a problem, well...well, there wouldn't be any problem at all, would there?

He felt her hand on his thigh again. She nibbled on his earlobe oh so gently. Her hand worked its way up his thigh.

Giving in would be the easy thing to do, the path of least resistance. And why not? He had already given in to the mayor's daughter once, anyway. That was where the real damage had been done. His spiritual journey had come to an end. He really didn't see that he was going to get any farther. In fact, he was losing ground. How crazy was it to keep on when he was losing ground? Very crazy, that was how crazy.

So how much more damage could it do if he were to play with her again? Or again and again repeatedly, if she wanted? What the heck?

***

Outside the hermit's shack, the ground started to ripple and rupple. The air itself shook, making the officers feel as if they were in an invisible mosh pit. Seven six-foot-tall badgers dressed in tuxedos came dancing across the clearing in a chorus line. The clouds formed themselves into a vision of the Swedish army. Nearby trees grew faces and began singing "My Old Kentucky Home" in three-part harmony, in Bob Dylan's voice.

In his office, the chairman was excited. "Yes, now we'll put an end to all this," he said.

The officers moved in. The ground was still rippling and ruppling, so their footing wasn't very good. It was slow going. They trudged on, falling down every few steps, but they finally made it.

The lead officer threw the door open and rushed inside, his fellow officers close behind.

The hermit broke away from the mayor's daughter and sat up. "Who are these people?" he asked in a voice that sounded like a woman with a high-pitched voice screaming as she fell out of a hot-air balloon at ten thousand feet.

"They're the police," the mayor's daughter said,

pulling the blanket up to cover herself. "But we're not doing anything illegal."

"That may be," the lead officer said. Then he added, in a more serious tone, "But we're not here officially as police officers."

Now, the mayor's daughter understood immediately what that meant. But the hermit missed the meaning completely. After living alone for half a century, he wasn't well practiced in understanding subtlety and nuances and shades of meaning. (You might think that what the officer said wasn't subtle, and you would be right. But to the hermit, it was.)

"You can't do this," the mayor's daughter said. "I won't let you."

"You can't do anything about it," the lead officer said. "Take him away, boys."

The other officers took the hermit by the arms and dragged him to the door. The lead officer noticed the hermit's coat. Curious, he took it off its peg and held it out at arm's length. "This thing is *hideous*!"

"What's going on?" the hermit asked.

"I'm sorry, mister," one of the officers said, "but you were in the wrong place at the wrong time."

"But I've been here for fifty daggone years! You people are the ones in the wrong place!"

"No," the officer said. He pointed to the mayor's daughter. "*She's* in the wrong place."

"I beg your pardon!" the mayor's daughter said. She was radiating so much anger and indignation that it gave the officers a painful rash.

"Look, miss," the lead officer said, "you know what's going on here. This is for the good of the party, and for your own good."

"What about *my* good?" the hermit asked.

"I guess there's not enough good to go around," the lead officer said.

CHAPTER FOURTEEN

The hermit had been drugged. When he woke up, he realized he was strapped to a bed that was somehow attached upside down to the ceiling of what appeared to be a large basement with a concrete floor.

He couldn't help but notice that it looked like the basement of the warehouse he had entered in the Seven Mischievous Elves, the basement where he had seen the mayor's daughter and the others playing pin the tail on the goldfish.

All he could see now, though, was another guy in the same predicament, about twenty feet away. "Hi," the hermit said.

The other guy, who might have been asleep, roused himself and looked at the hermit. "Hi."

"Where are we?"

"I don't know. The last thing I remember, I was playing bouncy-bouncy with this really wild girl I had met. Then I woke up, and I was here. Guys were making threats and stuff."

"Cute girl, wavy black hair, round little button nose?"

"Yeah."

"The mayor's daughter. She's a wild one, all right."

"Did you play bouncy-bouncy with her, too?" the guy asked.

"Once, a couple weeks ago. She came to see me again last night, and the police busted in on us."

"She came back for seconds?" The other guy's eyes were big and wide, impressed. If it had been possible, he would have gotten down on his knees and bowed down before the hermit and offered him the most reverend "I am not worthy" he could muster. Well, he could have still given him the "I am not worthy," but it's just not the same if you don't do the bowing routine along with it.

"Yeah," the hermit said. "I don't know why. I kept telling her no, but she kept insisting."

"Of course you told her no. You didn't want to end up here, like this."

"I didn't know anything about this place. I still don't know what's going on."

"Well, I'm not so sure myself," the other guy said. "I played with her and ended up here. She's been playing around a lot. I think someone might be trying to scare all the guys away from her, or something."

"I wish I had known," the hermit said.

"If you didn't know about this place, why did you tell her no? Are you married, or what?"

"No, I'm not married. The thing is, I'm a hermit. I live all by myself up on the mountainside."

"Oh, I see." He didn't see, but he thought that since this hermit guy apparently believed it was self-explanatory, he didn't want to ask for an explanation and therefore appear dumb.

"She came up to visit me," the hermit said. "She worked her feminine charms on me, and I gave in to temptation."

"Oh, women. They're evil."

"Yes, they are," the hermit said. And then, "No, they're not. She just wanted what she wanted, and I was just weak. That's the whole story. The police broke in and caught us in the act. When you get caught in the middle of playing bouncy-bouncy, you can't say, 'Oh, this isn't what it looks like.' There's only one thing that looks like playing bouncy-bouncy."

The other poor sap nodded slowly. (Yes, "other"—the hermit had now officially assumed the status of "poor sap" himself.) "That's rough, getting caught in the middle of it."

"You don't know the half of it, buddy," the hermit said. "They busted in right at the...well, I don't know how to say it, but...they came in right at the critical moment. I think I ruptured something."

The other poor sap cringed.

"I suppose it doesn't matter now," the hermit said. "I'll never use those particular parts again, anyway."

***

Meanwhile, the mayor's daughter was at the police station complaining. She had taken her complaint all the way up to the police chief. "Three of your officers busted in on my friend the hermit and dragged him out of his shack," she said. "For no reason at all. He didn't do anything wrong."

"Look, miss," the police chief said. "I don't know what you're talking about. We've never have any operations going on involving that hermit. I don't even know for sure whether he really exists."

"Oh, he exists, all right. He exists, and you've known all along that he was up there. You had your guys follow me, and they busted in on us."

The police chief suspected this must have been the work of the mayor's party chairman. Yeah, gracious living. And he sure was enjoying the heck out of that gold toilet paper dispenser.

"I'm sorry you were victimized by some hoodlums, miss. If you want to file a complaint, the desk sergeant would be happy to take your report."

The mayor's daughter was frustrated. This was going nowhere. It was corruption of the highest order, she thought, and she wasn't sure what to do about it if the police chief himself was stonewalling.

"What if I go to the news people with this?" she asked.

"What if you do?" the chief said. "Do you think they'll launch an investigation into police corruption and do a hard-hitting expose that'll cause public outrage and result in sweeping changes in the police department?"

"Well...maybe."

"I'll tell you what'll happen. The first thing they'll do is come to me and ask for a comment. I'll tell them that we had no case, absolutely no case whatsoever, that involved that hermit in any way. I'll tell them we received a report that he was apparently taken away by some officers, and we're investigating. We're taking the report very seriously. A few days later, I'll be able to announce that we've arrested a few guys for impersonating police officers. We're kinda sorta looking for the hermit, but we're not looking very hard because we're not sure he really exists, and if he does, we don't know that anything happened that we should be involved in.

That'll be the end of it, except that you'll have half—or maybe all of—the police force in the village mad at you. We don't want anything to happen to you while your dad is still the mayor, but after he's out of office, I don't know what those guys might do. You might end up locked in the basement of an abandoned warehouse somewhere, with no one knowing what became of you." The chief didn't know about the warehouse and didn't even want to know about that kind of thing. It was just an idea he happened, by coincidence, to pull out of thin air.

Lots of thoughts were racing through the mayor's daughter's head, racing and weaving around one another, making a lot of noise and competing for her attention. The police chief had been surprisingly frank, and she believed him. She wasn't likely to make a complaint go anywhere. She wasn't ready to give up on the idea completely, but it would be a good idea to see if she could think of other ways to deal with all this.

And the police chief thought of what he might ask the party chairman for next. He might like a gold statue of a wolf for his front yard. That would look way cool.

***

The party chairman came to see the hermit the next day. He entered with a spring in his step and a smile on his face. Oh, yeah, and a twinkle in his eye. We can't forget the twinkle.

"Hello, hermit," the chairman said.

"Who are you?" the hermit said.

"Let's just say I arranged for your accommodations

here," the chairman said.

"Mine, too?" the other poor sap said.

"Shut up," the chairman said. He turned back to the hermit. "Did you enjoy your little fling with the mayor's daughter?"

"I think I ruptured something when those guys busted in."

"That's too bad, but it doesn't matter. You won't be using those body parts anymore, anyway."

"Why am I here?"

"I'll tell you about that. See, the girl, the mayor's daughter, has been playing around with a lot of guys. We believe that's going to be a bad thing when the next election comes, so we want her to stop. Long story short, we came to the point where we figured we should just make all the guys scared to play with her. So this is what happens if you get caught."

"But I didn't know," the hermit said.

"Me neither," said the other poor sap.

"Well, now you both know."

"Does that mean we can go now?" the hermit asked.

"No, that's not how it works. Just between you and me, I think you're a likeable guy, and I'm sorry to see this happen to you. But you're here for the duration."

"The duration of what?"

"Of you."

"Am I here for the duration of him, too?" the other poor sap asked. "Because he's a lot older than…"

"Shut *up*!" the chairman snapped.

"Don't we get a court trial or something?" the hermit asked.

The chairman chuckled. "You don't understand. This isn't a criminal matter. "You haven't broken any laws. You just happened to cause a problem for us."

"It sounds to me as if the girl is the one causing problems," the hermit said.

"If you want to get right down to it, yes. The mayor's daughter is the one we're concerned about."

"So you could let me go," the hermit said.

"We could, but we won't. We don't want word to get around that we let someone go. We've reached the point where guys who play with the mayor's daughter have to disappear."

"But I won't tell anyone."

"Word could get out."

"How would word get out? I never talk to anyone!"

"No, you don't. And yet, here you are, hanging from the ceiling while she's out there somewhere, free to do whatever she's doing, as long as she's not trying to play bouncy-bouncy with some guy. I know it's not fair."

"It's not fair," the hermit said.

***

Later, some guys came in and got the two poor saps down off the ceiling.

***

The party chairman was pleased with himself. The problem of mayor's daughter was behind him now, and it was going to be smooth sailing to the next election. He was quite pleased to order the statue of the golden wolf for the police chief. He had encountered some confusion trying to get the pose just right, and then the guy who was making the statue wasn't sure how big to make it, and for some reason he wanted to make a whole scene out of it with—get this—with dancing goldfish, of all things.

Whoever heard of dancing goldfish?

The chairman got the guy straightened out, though, and the statue would be delivered soon. Those problems, the ones with the statue guy, they weren't nearly as bad as the problems with the mayor's daughter.

Yes, life was good.

***

And the mayor? Well, he was just bopping along, doing his usual mayor stuff. As long as no one was getting all up in his face yelling at him, he was assuming everything was okay.

***

They moved the hermit to a small, private cell a couple days later. It was in a dungeon, deep inside the earth, cold and clammy and somewhat dank. They let him have his books and journals and things to write with because there was no need to be so mean as to take everything away from him. However, they didn't allow him to keep his subscription to *Modern Hermit* magazine. It would be too much trouble to have it delivered.

After the hermit became acclimated to his new home, the mysterious stranger paid him a visit. The hermit woke up from a nap, and there he was, the mysterious stranger, lurking in the corner. It was hard for the hermit to make him out at first, in the dim lighting, what with the dark robe the mysterious stranger was wearing.

"What?" the hermit said. "Who are you?"

"I'm the mysterious stranger. We've had a couple little chit-chats before, remember?"

"Yeah, I remember. You told me to do the very thing I did that got me locked up in here. You'll understand if I'm not thrilled to see you come back again."

"There you go, blaming your problems on other people. So much of that going around these days."

"Well, you know, I do have to question why you would encourage me to do something like that."

"It's like the mayor's daughter said. Everybody needs to play bouncy-bouncy occasionally. It's good for your physical and your emotional well-being. If you deny it, your life gets all out of balance. You live in your body, so you have to provide it what it needs."

"Now's a fine time to tell me. It's too late for me to do anything about it now."

"Look, dude, you should have figured it out long before I came along. You should have figured it out before you became a hermit."

"When I became a hermit, I was too young to figure out stuff like that."

"This might not be the way you had expected it would all end, but I have to say it's pretty much the same thing as being a hermit, anyway. It shouldn't be that bad."

"No, it's not the same thing as being a hermit. Not at all."

"Well, it's a lot like being a hermit."

"No," the hermit insisted, "it's not anything like being a hermit."

"Maybe not, but if you've been a hermit for all that

time, this shouldn't be very bad."

"That's a heck of a thing to say."

"What do you expect? That I'm going to come in here and tell you how to escape?"

"No. I'm just wondering if you had some reason for showing up here besides acting like a jerk."

"No, I don't think so, not really. The main thing I wanted to say is, I hope all this has taught you a lesson."

***

The mayor's daughter continued reading about hermits. She had a lot of time for reading because it was still impossible for her to find playmates.

She began toying with the idea of going to hermit school. She didn't think she would actually become a hermit. The subject, though, was fascinating. So she got on the Internet and found the web site for hermit school. She looked over the curriculum and the pictures of the facilities and the biographies of the instructors.

She noticed the school was fully certified.

She requested literature about the school. They sent a nice, professional-looking booklet and all sorts of forms, and so on. She filled out the application and did the aptitude tests and sent them in, not serious about it but just curious to see whether they would accept her.

They did. The president of the school himself sent her a personal letter saying he thought she was one of the most outstanding prospects he had seen in many years. Her aptitude test scores were so high that he got dizzy looking at them. He hoped she would come to school, and he looked forward to seeing her in class.

Wow, she thought. She didn't know that they sent every applicant the same letter.

"They think I'm an outstanding prospect," she told her best friend.

"I can't believe you're even thinking about it," the best friend said.

"I'm interested in hermit stuff. Why wouldn't I think about it?"

"Are you interested enough to give up everything and go live by yourself for the rest of your life?"

"That's not the point. I just want to learn about hermitism. Maybe I'll become an expert and write a book or make a documentary film. I think it would be fun to make a documentary film about being a hermit."

The mayor's daughter arranged for the easy financing, packed her stuff, and went off to hermit school. She was indeed a good student, the best student many of the instructors had ever seen. "You remind me of a fella who was here about fifty years ago, back in my first year of teaching," one of the old-timers told her, an instructor who was going to retire after the current school year was over. "He was mostly a pretty good student, did poorly in a couple of courses but was very dedicated, as I recall. Funny thing. He liked to hide. He would hide in the classroom during class. You wouldn't see him, but you knew he was there somewhere. He just had a thing for hiding." The instructor paused, musing. "I wonder whatever became of him."

"I'm sure he did okay for himself," the mayor's daughter said.

She graduated with an A+ average, the best performance of any student the school had ever seen. And she had to think: It would be an unthinkable waste of talent not to become a hermit. What if Mickey Mantle had never become a ball player? What if Ernest Hemingway had never become a writer? What if Mister Rogers had never become a sweater model?

On the other hand, she simply wasn't prepared to give up bouncy-bouncy for the rest of her life. She had done well in the courses on how to put thoughts of women out of your mind, but she wasn't going to have a problem with thinking about women, anyway. The school simply didn't see very many female students, and they had never considered that those few female students would be better served by learning how to put thoughts of men out of their minds.

The mayor's daughter had never learned that. She had, in fact, occasionally been able to sneak away somewhere private with one of the male students. They were, generally, all too willing to indulge in the charms of a lovely young lady, considering that after graduation they were facing a lifetime of going without. (What about the weird phenomena? Some were reported, but the school administrators had no idea what was causing it.)

She eventually decided she would try living as a hermit for two or three years. That wouldn't be too long to bear, she believed, and it would give her some experience. That way, when she wrote her book or shot her documentary film, or whatever she decided to do, it would be really, truly authentic. She was sure she could go without her bouncy-bouncy that long if it meant she would be able to put together a way-cool project about hermits.

She contacted hermit school and asked them to set

her up with an apprenticeship so she could begin her new life. They thought the hermit—our hermit—might be a good mentor for her to stay with, but they couldn't get in touch with him. It was almost as if he had disappeared altogether.

A few weeks later, the mayor's daughter left for Peru, where Harold Recluse lived in a nifty two-room shack up on a mountaintop with a striking view. Harold was known far and wide throughout hermit circles for developing several "speed meditation" techniques that instructors at hermit school had adopted in their courses. He didn't normally accept apprentices, but when they told him what an outstanding student the mayor's daughter had been, and how much potential she showed, he had to agree to take her.

Yes, it was going to be a wonderful adventure. The mayor's daughter boarded her plane, all ingly and tingly with excitement. She flew to Peru with no doubt in her mind that all her plans were going to work out very well.

***

And the hermit? Well, after the election, a new guy was mayor (due in large part to rumors about stuff that may or may not have happened to the poor saps who were taken away after playing with the mayor's daughter—something the old mayor's party hadn't considered in their zeal to solve the problem, but the stories spread, and people voted accordingly). And he, the new mayor, figured this scruffy old fella who was locked away down there, down in the dungeon...well, he hadn't really done anything, had he? Sure, it was disgusting to think of a wrinkled-up old geezer like him playing bouncy-bouncy with a lovely, young lady like the former mayor's daughter, but it certainly wasn't illegal. Besides, he—the new mayor, that is—he might need all the dungeon space he could muster up, just in case he had to deal with political dissidents or something. He had no particular plans in that regard, mind you—no, not really, but you never know.

And besides, on top of that, it would *look good* if he let the old man go, right? The previous mayor had obviously locked him up simply for personal reasons. It was an egregious abuse of power.

The new mayor could right a wrong. He would be a hero, and it would be a sappy, heartwarming story.

The public would love it. They would eat it up the way a six-year-old eats up a big, fluffy ball of pink, sticky cotton candy. They would eat it up the way a porcupine eats up a hot bowl of macaroni and cheese with bacon bits sprinkled over the top.

Mmmmm...bacon.

And so, amid much fanfare and publicity, the new mayor released the hermit from the dungeon. He released the other poor sap, too...was it just one other guy still in the dungeon, or more? I lost track. Anyway, the new mayor let all the poor saps out of the dungeon, however many there were.

It was a festive event, with lots of publicity and a marching band and parade floats and unicorns. (The parade floats were left over from the Village's Annual Celebration Under Opulent, Ubiquitous Stars. They were sort of in a state of disrepair, and covered with mold and graffiti, so they weren't really all that festive. But they were parade floats.)

The hermit made a little speech to thank the new mayor and posed for pictures—not that he wanted to, but if that was what it took to get free, that was what he would do. And the other poor sap(s) posed and gave his (their) speech(es) as well.

Then the hermit made his way back up to the mountainside. He set about doing some repair work on his shack because it had been sitting out there unattended for, what, something like, oh, maybe three and a half years, close to four, or thereabouts. A few boards had come loose and whatnot.

But before he was able to settle back into his way of life, he had visitors. These were different sorts of visitors, though, from the mayor's daughter and the mysterious stranger and the police officers working for the party chairman.

No, these visitors were people like magazine writers and book publishers and movie directors who wanted to tell his story. They were people like talk show producers who wanted to book him for television and radio interviews.

They were people like cell phone service providers and sunscreen manufacturers and gas mask designers hoping to sign up the hermit to endorse their products. Why would a hermit who was famous for nothing more than getting unjustly locked up endorse products? Who cared? His story had captivated the public's imagination, and he was becoming a celebrity! That was what mattered.

With all this attention, it became apparent to the hermit that he wasn't going to be allowed to be a hermit anymore. If he were younger, it would just be one of those "fifteen minutes" kinda things. People would eventually lose interest and forget about him, and he would be able to go back to his hermitosity. (Hermitosity...nice word. I wish I had thought of it earlier in the story so I could have used it more.) But old as he was, he had to allow as how his fifteen minutes of fame might last longer than he himself would. It seemed morbid to be thinking that way, but he believed it was best to be realistic.

And besides that, well, he had to admit that he was enjoying all this new stuff that was happening. Women were throwing themselves at him. Yes, throwing themselves!

So he figured he might as well embrace all this stuff. He might as well become one with the hype and the hoopla and hullabaloo and excitement. Make the most of it. Enjoy it.

The hermit signed up with one of the dozens of business managers who had been knocking on his door. And the manager hired the fancy New York PR firm to handle publicity. The hermit was on his way!

A talented, good-looking, up-and-coming novelist wrote his story. Noted film director Werner Herzog made a movie about him. The endorsements, and checks therefrom, rolled in. He appeared on *The Diane Chatter Show* and *Later than You Want to Stay Awake with Chuck Palaver.* He rolled out his own line of pet turtle accessories. He starred in a reality show. He cut a pop music CD. And all over—not just in the village, but all over the country—stores were full of hermit merchandise: T-shirts, video games, posters, calendars, coffee mugs, cell phones, mouse pads, neckties, lunch boxes. For some reason, there was hermit duct tape. At Halloween, kids dressed as the hermit.

He lived out the rest of his days in a big house at the edge of the village, surrounded by beautiful women of all descriptions. He ate gourmet food and drank exotic wine at the dinner parties he gave every day, and everyone agreed that to be invited to one of these affairs was the very pinnacle of social accomplishment.

THE END

PS: At the hermit's shack, the old, long-neglected and forgotten shack up on the mountainside, a chipmunk nosed the door open. He stepped in and saw the coat. Although he wasn't able to pull it off the peg and hold it out at arm's length, he could see it clearly enough to think, "That thing's *hideous*!"

If you liked *The Hermit*, try these other books by Ray Holland:

Goliath: It's a tale of good and evil, of trust and suspicion, of the power of love and loyalty. Little Goliath and his friends face adversity from within themselves, from one another, and from the forces of evil as they work to foil the Neuralgia Sisters' nefarious plot to achieve world domination.

Open Stage: A mysterious, alluring woman, a hyperactive, funny little man, and a very strange business deal leads Gilbert Ragwater to learn a few things about himself. It's a coming-of-age story for those of us with arrested development.

The Hookie-Pookie Man: His mother was from Earth, and his father was from another planet. He doesn't fit in anywhere, but he knows a woman of similar origin is out there somewhere—and he's determined to find her.

Soft White Underbelly: Join Thor and his friends as they overthrow the government from the comfort of Thor's home, go to a yard sale and find a weapon so powerful that it can't be used, encounter a soul-stealing snack machine at the airport, take inventory of everything on the planet, circulate a petition for a Better America, embark on a plot to assassinate Satan...and more. Much, much more!

www.ingramcontent.com/pod-product-compliance
Lightning Source LLC
LaVergne TN
LVHW091039080826
845145LV00002B/559

* 9 7 8 0 6 1 5 2 7 9 1 7 6 *